ME AND BANKSY

TANYA LLOYD KYI

PUFFIN

an imprint of Penguin Random House Canada Young Readers, a Penguin
Random House Company

First published 2020

1 2 3 4 5 6 7 8 9 10

Text copyright © 2020 by Tanya Lloyd Kyi

Jacket design: John Martz
Jacket images: googly eyes © MirageC/Getty Images; wall © Katsumi
Murouchi/Getty Images

*Publisher's note: This book is a work of fiction. Names, characters, places
and incidents either are the product of the author's imagination or are used
fictitiously, and any resemblance to actual persons living or dead, events, or
locales is entirely coincidental.*

Manufactured in Canada

Library and Archives Canada Cataloguing in Publication

Title: Me and Banksy / Tanya Lloyd Kyi.
Names: Kyi, Tanya Lloyd, 1973- author.
Identifiers: Canadiana (print) 20190110481 | Canadiana (ebook)
2019011049X | ISBN 9780735266919 (hardcover) |
ISBN 9780735266926 (EPUB)
Classification: LCC PS8571.Y52 M42 2020 | DDC jC813/.6—dc23

Library of Congress Control Number: 2019939213

www.penguinrandomhouse.ca

Penguin
Random House
PUFFIN CANADA

For Matthew, my anti-authoritarian son.

The bad artists imitate, the great artists steal.

—~~PABLO PICASSO~~

—~~BANKSY~~

—DOMINICA RIVERS

CHAPTER ONE
SAY *FROMAGE*

GRANDMA GEORGINA and I sit on the patio at La Patisserie, where she treats Mom and me to brunch every Sunday. My mother is late.

"She inherited my looks but your grandfather's brains." George sighs.

Grandma Georgina prefers me to call her George, especially in public. She says the word *grandma* nullifies the hundreds of dollars per month she spends on salon coloring, and there's no sense wasting cash on an unnecessary label.

"I've got something special for you," she says, pulling her leather shoulder bag onto her lap. Every week, she brings me a different book from her gallery's gift shop.

I hand back last week's hardcover, a collection of still-life paintings by Mary Pratt. On the cover, red currant jelly glistens like blood in glass dessert cups.

"Oooh . . . what did you think, Dominica?" George lifts the book toward her carefully, as if the jelly might spill.

"Ridiculously sad."

"The essay about her baby twins dying?"

"I'm scarred forever. You should give me happier books."

"But you can see the devastation in her work, can't you?" George waves her hands rather dramatically, and I slide her water glass out of danger.

"You can. Even when it's a painting of fruit," I admit.

"Isn't that incredible?"

The way she says it, I'm not entirely sure if George is talking about Mary Pratt or me.

"Well, this week, I brought something completely different," she says. "Something—"

We're distracted by a silver Lexus zooming up the street. My mother swerves into a parking spot across from our patio. She hops from her car before the wheels have quite stopped rolling, checks the meter, and clicks a few buttons on her cell. As we watch, she shakes her phone and pushes a few more buttons. Then she scrabbles in the bottom of her purse for change.

Her purse is the size of an ocean-going vessel. Trying to find anything in there will be hopeless.

I can see her frustration building. It's as if her dark hair is curling more and more tightly.

"I'll go and help," I say.

George puts her hand on my arm. "Never mind, Dominica. She'll figure it out eventually."

Which is true. Mom disappears into a store and reappears a minute later with gourmet chocolate bars in one hand and a collection of coins in the other. After she feeds the meter, she jaywalks across the street, waving prettily at the black Jag that almost hits her.

"Tuck this in your backpack for later," George says, passing me her newest book selection. "It's quite subversive."

Before I can ask what "subversive" means, Mom drops into the chair beside mine.

"What a morning!"

She may not be the most organized, and she doesn't always

make the best decisions, but Mom has a smile like the whipped cream on top of my *chocolat chaud*. As soon as her dimples appear, I want to kiss her. I can tell it works the same way on George.

Mom gives us each a chocolate bar, which also helps. I tuck mine into my pack as our favorite waiter appears.

"Pierre, darling," George says, motioning him lower so she can pat his cheek.

Once that little ritual's over, we order our meals. Then George turns to me, clasps her hands together, and says, "Well, girl who inherited both my brains *and* my looks, what's new in eighth grade?"

"Nothing much," I say. "I have a project due this week."

"For what class?" Mom asks.

If she were a different type of mom, she'd already know the answer. But our Sunday brunches are an update for her as much as for George. Which might be why George insists that she turn up every week.

"Ethics. We have to write about a privacy or security technology that's changing the world."

"And what did you choose?" George asks.

"Drones."

Mom wrinkles her nose. "Horrible things. Don't they drop bombs?"

I nod. "But you should see all the other crazy stuff they do. Artists are using them to create aerial ballets, circus performances, multimedia shows . . ."

"What does that have to do with privacy, dear?" George asks.

I grin sheepishly. "I got a little distracted while I was researching. But I have a few more days to work on it."

Mom yawns.

"They can also deliver pizza to your door, minutes after you order," I tell her.

"How wonderful." George turns to Mom. "Perhaps they could deliver your canapés, darling."

"As if my human servers aren't trouble enough," Mom says.

She and her best friend own a catering company, and she's always complaining about finding good staff.

I pick up the bread basket and swing it gently through the air toward her. "More bread, madam?" I ask in robot-voice.

Mom snorts.

Pierre returns, setting down our breakfast plates. He lifts George's napkin from beside her cutlery and flicks it elegantly into her lap before offering a twist of freshly ground pepper.

George sighs happily. "Let's not replace Pierre with a flying robot quite yet," she whispers as he leaves.

Mom, meanwhile, is examining a piece of sausage on the end of her fork. "Now *this* is a world-changing invention," she says. Then she eats it.

I'm having mascarpone French toast, also world-changing, and George is nibbling on poached eggs and fruit.

"How was your morning, Carol?" George asks, between strawberries.

"A wedding rehearsal dinner for thirty guests tonight. We're completely in the weeds. Soon we have the wedding itself, *and* we're catering a conference on the same day."

"You've been busy," George says. "Dominica tells me you've met a new friend, too."

4

Which is a complete lie. Mom's been out with her new "friend" quite often lately, leaving me to my own devices, but...

"George, I never said that!"

When Mom's eyes flit to me, I give her an innocent shrug. I have no idea how my grandma knows these things. It's as if she can smell gossip.

"My new friend is Frank. He's a lawyer," Mom says.

"*Ooh la la*. Does he yoga with you as well?"

"Yoga is not a verb." Mom rolls her eyes.

She *did* meet Frank at yoga, though. Maybe George is psychic.

"Is he divorced?" George asks next.

Definitely psychic.

Things go on like this until we finish our meals, George pays the bill, and we collect our jackets. As we pass the host and his podium, I spot a camera above the front door. Ever since we started this privacy and security unit in our ethics class, I've been extra aware of cameras. Now I notice them everywhere.

I pause to wave at this one. If someone has to watch that video feed, they have the most boring job ever. They deserve a little encouragement.

On the sidewalk, George kisses us each on both cheeks, as if eating at a French café has turned us into French people. She holds my hands in hers for longer than necessary afterward, and looks me directly in the eyes.

"Everything okay?" she asks.

"Perfect," I say.

At that moment, it's completely true.

———

HOLDEN: Help!

ME: ?

HOLDEN: Stuck in a dungeon, can't get out.

ME: Does "boy who cried wolf" mean anything to you?

HOLDEN: Would it help if I said ur a genius?

ME: That's been scientifically established. Your opinion isn't necessary.

HOLDEN: One day, when ur undercover and someone blows ur identity, exposing you to lurking assassins, I'll leap in front of the bullet for you

ME: brt

It's not as if I have anything else to do. George has a meeting with a gallery client, Mom's gone back to work, and—even though you'd think I'd be used to it by now—I don't love being home by myself.

It seems I'm free to help with gaming emergencies.

I bike the few blocks to Holden's house, a Victorian mansion his architect parents have restored. Not renovated. Restored. That means they've polished the dark wood wainscoting, replaced the shredded original hardwood with "salvaged boards," and otherwise spent hundreds of thousands of dollars to make everything look perfectly old. You can practically smell years of roast turkey dinners, see petticoat-clad girls skipping down the stairs, and hear an eccentric aunt scribbling her man-uscript in the attic.

I knock lightly on the French doors at the back, and Holden's mom waves me inside. She's on the phone, her lac-quered blonde hair tucked behind one ear.

"Drink? Snack?" she mouths.

When I shake my head, she points me downstairs. I find Holden on the leather couch in the basement media room, slouched in a nest of blankets. There's an open bag of potato chips on the coffee table, and the air smells of socks and morning breath.

"How long have you been playing?"

He jumps at the sound of my voice and pulls himself upright. Then he launches into a long explanation of his problem. I have to look away from the screen so I don't get dizzy while his character races over rockslides and around traps, the view tilting and turning.

"I'm great today, thanks for asking," I say.

No response.

"Yes, it *is* nice outside. I had brunch with my mom and my grandma."

"Almost there," he says.

"My grandma's having an alien baby."

"Here! This is the issue."

He points to a wall panel emblazoned with three symbols. "I have to make all three of them light up at the same time, and I found the horseshoe—"

"That's an omega."

"And the funny-shaped n—"

"That's pi."

"But I can't find this loopy thing."

"Theta."

"I'm stuck until I solve it! I need your puzzle skills."

"Isn't this why they invented Google?"

"That's cheating," he says.

So while it's cheating to search for the answer, it's okay to call me for help. This makes absolutely no sense, but whatever. I brush chip crumbs off a couch cushion, sit down beside him, and reach for the controller.

This sort of thing has always been easy for me—it takes only a minute to figure out the puzzle. Theta glows once I shoot omega and pi in quick succession. But no escape route appears.

"What's all this red stuff?"

"It blows up if you shoot it. Press X," Holden says.

I hand back the controller. "Shoot omega and pi, then shoot theta once it glows, then hit the red stuff while all three are still lit up."

After a flurry of clicking, the bass of an explosion shakes the room. On screen, the wall crumbles to reveal a gate, which screeches open.

"You're officially the best ever," Holden says (without looking at me, because he's already running from the dungeon).

"Well, now that I've saved the world, I guess I'll go finish my ethics project." I take a handful of chips for the ride.

"Wait," he says as I reach the doorway.

I pause.

"Will your family accept your grandma's alien baby, or will she have to give it up for adoption?"

I throw a chip at his head, but it falls disappointingly short.

I'm upstairs and almost out the door when Holden's mom catches me.

"Dominica! Are you leaving already? I was hoping you might distract Holden. Take him out somewhere."

Ms. LaClaire and I have had variations of this conversation about a thousand times before.

"He won't go. He's deep in his game."

She clicks her tongue and I wait for the rest, the part where she asks what activities Holden might enjoy.

"He and I used to be so close, honey." She sighs.

When he was a kid, five or six years old, Holden was the blue-eyed, freckled star of a show called *Me in the Middle*. He went on to guest appearances on some even more successful shows. But by sixth grade, when we started hanging out, he'd stopped acting and quit his after-school dance, music, and voice classes. He'd sort of stopped everything.

Which is what Ms. LaClaire wrings her hands about every time she talks to me.

Thankfully, her phone buzzes.

"Sorry," she mouths.

I slip out the door while I have the chance.

CHAPTER TWO
SECURITY CHECK

WHEN I GET OFF the elevator on Monday morning, Holden's leaning against the security desk in my lobby. He's attempting to chat up our building concierge, Lou, a retired police officer with a brush cut and a scowl to match.

Lou doesn't chat.

"Dangerous world out there, Dominica," he says when I appear.

"Thanks."

"You have a great day, Lou," Holden says.

Once the two of us are outside, we grin at one another. We have the same conversation with Lou every day before school.

Personally, I don't know how the world could be dangerous on this particular morning. It's late April, and a carpet of fallen cherry blossoms swirls around us on the sidewalk as we hurry west. The Granville Street traffic fades to a background hum. It's as if we're alone in the world.

Our hands bump together and, for a moment, Holden links his pinky in mine. It's nice, and it feels like exactly what we should be doing in the middle of a cherry blossom storm. It doesn't mean anything, though. Or maybe it does? Holden and I have been friends for almost three years and it's hard to figure out where our boundaries are. Or where we want them to be. I might be okay with more than linked pinkies, but I have no idea what Holden thinks.

We're halfway to Saanvi's house when he stops abruptly.

"What?"

"Forgot my device."

"Again?"

We all had trouble remembering our school ID tags for a few weeks last year, after the new system was installed. But I swear Holden has a subconscious aversion to his. He calls it his device, as in "tracking device." Saanvi's tried to explain that it only lets the office and our families know when we arrive and when we leave. Plus it uses radio frequencies, not GPS.

None of that seems to have helped him.

There's no time to discuss it now. We half-jog back toward his house, grab his tag, and then turn around and retrace our steps. I have to prod him along. He doesn't care if we're late, but I do. Even the thought of Mr. Nowak growling at me while I slink into homeroom gives me a stomachache.

When we get to Saanvi's place, she's already waiting outside, bouncing from one foot to the other. Her standard school uniform—blue blazer, white shirt, and pleated plaid skirt—flaps a little with every bounce.

Saanvi lives in a huge house on the corner of Beverly Crescent, with her parents, her older brother and his wife, and her grandma. This morning, her grandma's watching from the door. She blows us a kiss and calls something I don't understand.

The rest of Saanvi's family was born here, but her grandma

grew up in India. Even though she's fluent in English, she seems to think Holden and I speak Hindi. I kind of love that.

When I try to blow her a return kiss, Saanvi bats my hand down and tugs me toward school.

"I've been waiting seriously forever!" she says.

"Holden's fault."

"Obviously."

We fall into an elbow-jostling, forearm-brushing line across the sidewalk as we fast-walk the rest of the way. Holden tells us the latest in gaming news, while Saanvi and I compare bracelets. Hers is a gorgeous gold chain; mine is a woven-hemp piece of ridiculousness I found at a garage sale. George would probably make me burn it, but I love the intricate knots and the tiny turquoise beads woven through the strings.

The warning bell rings just as we get to the school grounds. We take the front stairs two at a time, burst through the double doors, and almost collide with our principal, who's leading a group of men in business suits. Potential donors, probably.

"As I was saying . . . state-of-the-art facilities." Ms. Plante puts a hand on Holden's shoulder and steers him toward the men. Saanvi and I follow a careful step behind.

"And here are some of our promising young students," Ms. Plante says. "This is Holden LaClaire. You may know his mother, from LaClaire Design? And Saanvi Agarwal, whose father sits on city council. And this is Dominica Rivers."

There's a dangling pause at the end of her sentence, where my family qualifications should be. She could easily mention

George's gallery, but I get the feeling our principal isn't an art fan.

"We pride ourselves on creating a safe, nurturing environment in which our students can explore their talents."

She sounds like a walking brochure. The suit guys seem to be lapping it up, though.

"As it says on the emblem outside: *securitas genera victoria*. Security breeds success. Those words guide all our decisions here at Mitchell Academy."

The motto is another of Ms. Plante's additions to the school, along with the ID tags and the cameras. She's a security fanatic. Holden says she was probably a prison guard before she got this job.

One of the men turns in a slow circle, gazing up at the high, arched ceiling with its gold-accented mural.

"When was the school built?"

"In 1922. Several years ago, the Mitchell Foundation bought a second campus to serve as our senior school. This original building now houses grades six through eight."

She skips over all the details I love. The Mitch was created by an eccentric oil painter named Eugenie Mitchell. When she died, she left all her money to create a school for gifted kids.

"... nearly one hundred percent graduation, and a nonexistent crime rate." Ms. Plante is officially gushing now.

If our principal has her own personal genius, it's fundraising. George reads the parent newsletter every month, and she says that since Ms. Plante arrived a couple years ago, the school has been receiving more donations and achieving better ratings than ever before.

As the second bell rings, Ms. Plante turns to us and claps her hands. "Off to class, everyone." She smiles brightly.

This is entirely for show, because her genius definitely does *not* lie in the cheerful encouragement of students.

We hurry to homeroom before she can show her true colors.

Holden and I have ethics after homeroom. It's my favorite class, entirely because of the teacher. Ms. Sutton is a small, gray-haired whirlwind in a sack dress and ballerina flats.

"Hurry and get seated. Lots to cover!" she calls. "We're going to embark on something new."

I slide into my desk and pull out my notebook, reaching across the aisle to poke Holden. It wouldn't kill him to take a few notes of his own, instead of borrowing mine. But he yawns and leans back in his chair. Miranda, in the desk behind his, begins playing with his curls. As always, she's wearing tights and high heels with her uniform. Today, her heels are gold and glittery.

She twists a strand of his hair around her finger.

Ugh.

Miranda's the editor of the student blog at The Mitch, but apparently she has other interests as well.

Ana Kavanaugh, math and science prodigy, literally skips past us on her way to a desk in the front row. She's so tiny she looks as if she's playing dress-up in her school uniform.

"We're going to focus on world-changers this month," Ms. Sutton says. Then she pauses as Josh Plante, Max Lin, and a gang of their fellow athletes/orangutans shove and shout their way to their desks at the back.

". . . a major project," she continues. Her smile seems tight, though, and I peer at her more closely. For once, she doesn't have her usual, I-meditated-for-hours-this-morning glow. She has a little crease between her eyebrows and she's playing with her rings as she speaks.

Marcus, a pimply guy in the front row, raises his hand. "Aren't we going to finish the privacy and security unit? What about our projects?"

Ms. Sutton smiles tightly. "You can hand in your projects next week, but we'll leave the rest of the unit for another time. Today, we're going to focus on—"

She stops when Ana thrusts a hand in the air, so high she might attract lightning.

"May I ask why, Ms. Sutton?"

"Why what, Ana?"

"Why we're switching topics?"

Maybe I notice it only because I've already seen the tension in Ms. Sutton's expression. Her eyes flit ever so briefly to the camera in the corner of our room.

Partway through seventh grade, after some thefts from lockers, the small black globes appeared in the hallways and classrooms. They were for our safety, Ms. Plante said. There were parent meetings about it, but everyone seemed to agree that extra security was necessary.

Ms. Sutton gives her head a tiny shake. "There's a lot to cover this term," she says. "We got sidetracked, and we're going to move on to something fun."

When no one else interrupts, she nods briskly. "I want to see an in-depth research project about someone who inspires you. Someone who's challenged society's ethics, or someone

15

who's changed the way you personally look at the world. You can choose an artist, a scientist, a philosopher. The options are endless." With that last word, she whirls a hand in the air, as if she's stirring the universe.

Ana sticks her hand up again, practically dislocating a shoulder.

"Will there be a presentation component, Ms. Sutton?"

"There are full requirements listed in the handout," Ms. Sutton says, passing papers to each row. "I want a four-page written report, an oral presentation to the class, and a creative project done in tribute to your subject. This can take whatever form you'd like. Be bold."

I glance over to see what Holden thinks of this new assignment. He has his eyes closed. Because he's receiving a head massage from Miranda.

I throw up a little in my mouth.

"You'll have four weeks, so use your time wisely," Ms. Sutton says. "Any other questions?"

Ana. Of course.

"Should the four pages be double-spaced?"

She's kind of like Hermione Granger, without the redeeming magical qualities. Most days, she makes me want to bang my head against my desk. She's always asking me to join a study group, or cofound a club, or sign up for a fundraiser, but she's so obsessive, I can't handle her for more than ten minutes at a time.

Last year, she borrowed my humanities notes after she was away sick one day. And instead of giving me my own pages back afterward, she gave me a new copy, color-coded in four ink varieties. She said my notes were "only adequate," so she'd improved them, in case Mr. Lee ever asked to see our binders.

Now that I think about it, maybe only five minutes at a time.

At least she seems to have finished with her questions, for now.

"Let's start with some research," Ms. Sutton says. "Pull out your laptops if you need them."

I already know my topic. Since the minute I paged through the book George gave me yesterday morning, I was in love. It seems like complete serendipity that Ms. Sutton would assign a project about inspirational people just as I've discovered someone incredible: Banksy.

I find an entry about him on a biography website.

The anonymous artist known as Banksy is a painter and film director originally based in Britain, whose pieces often comment on political or social issues. He is known for his intricate stencil work in public spaces. While Banksy's identity remains unknown, he has gained international acclaim for his work on streets, walls, and buildings throughout Europe, North America, and the Middle East.

I shake my head, still amazed about the anonymous part. At first, this guy was basically a criminal, spray-painting walls in England. But Banksy is such an original artist, even his graffiti drew attention. Now he's famous. And he's brilliant.

I flip through the examples online. Even as I smile, my heart cracks. He has this way of making it obvious that people can be wonderful *and* people can be horrible.

There's a painting from the wall of a youth club in England. It shows a man and a woman with their arms wrapped around one another, as if they're about to kiss. But they're *actually* looking over one another's shoulders to check messages on their phones.

As I said: brilliant.

I would love to be an artist one day. I've been taking drawing and painting lessons for years, not to mention devouring George's weekly book selections. Ms. Crofton, our art teacher at The Mitch, says my paintings have "potential." But all of these real artists have vision. They have their own strange ways of seeing the world and then putting it on canvas. Or on concrete, in Banksy's case.

I don't have that sort of vision.

George says no one has vision when they're thirteen, and I'll discover mine one day. That seems doubtful. Especially when I look at all the things Banksy has to say. How does he fit so much meaning into a few spray-painted shapes?

He did one of his most famous pieces in a place where massive security cameras watched the street. I guess in England, security cameras are called CCTV—which means closed-circuit television. Banksy painted huge white words on the side of the building: *One Nation Under CCTV*. And even though he painted directly underneath the cameras, he somehow didn't get caught.

I study the photo, trying to figure out how he did it. Did he cover up the lenses somehow? Or was there a blind spot directly beneath the cameras? It's impossible to tell—I'd need more photos, taken from other angles.

As I start scribbling notes for my essay, I'm distracted by Ana. She's standing beside her desk, precisely arranging a still life of her notebook, a pencil, and an owl-shaped eraser. I don't have a PixSnappy account, but Saanvi has shown me enough posts—I can guess what Ana's next one is going to say. Something like, "Baby owl's helping with my assignment today!" Then she'll add a string of animal emojis and smiley faces.

My mother has a social media phobia. She says I'm not allowed a single account until I'm sixteen. But even if I *were* allowed to have PixSnappy, I might have to boycott the entire site because of Ana's posts.

I turn back to my laptop and skim a "Top 10 Banksy" list, then another biography website. Some of my favorite pieces are the silliest ones, but not in Ana's baby-owl way. Once, Banksy snuck into the elephant pen at the London Zoo and wrote this on the wall: *I want out. This place is too cold. Keeper smells. Boring, boring, boring.*

That's exactly how an elephant must feel at the London Zoo. And who doesn't love a graffiti artist who can talk to elephants?

There are even more reasons I'm obsessed with him . . .

"Do you have a subject in mind, Dominica?"

Ms. Sutton has the tiniest hint of a British accent, and my name (actually a reminder that my mom and dad began their love affair in a Dominican Republic resort) always sounds better when she says it.

"I'm going to choose . . ."

At the front of the class, Ana waves her hand in the air. "Ms. Sutton! I can't pick one. I was considering Rachel Carson, because she basically began the entire environmental movement? But I also love Malala? How can I choose? I want to do my project on someone who really speaks to the power of the female experience?"

I happen to catch Holden's eye. (The head massage seems to be over, finally.) He makes the universal sign for choking, and I feel slightly better.

"A paragraph from each of you, outlining your project, by Thursday!" Ms. Sutton calls as the bell rings for morning break.

I have one last scrap of humanities homework to finish, so I duck into the library during the break, choose a table at the back of the room, and open my laptop. The place is completely deserted—not even the librarian seems to be around.

Which is a good thing, I decide, because it appears I've been wearing my shirt inside out ALL MORNING! The embroidered Mitchell Academy crest is scratching against my skin. I can't believe I didn't notice. I can't believe Holden and Saanvi didn't notice.

I scan the room; there's still no one here. Quickly, I whip off my shirt, flip it, and tug it back on. Then I set off to find Holden and Saanvi and complain. What good are friends if they don't warn you about wardrobe malfunctions?

CHAPTER THREE
EXCAVATIONS

A BUZZING NOISE. I sit bolt upright, heart pounding. I'm on my couch, surrounded by sketches of Holden. I was trying to capture his trademark smirk. Beneath the drawings are a bunch of scribbled notes for my Banksy project. Late-afternoon sun streams through the living room windows. I shake my head and rub the sleep from my eyes. I got back from school, made myself a snack, and started my home-work, but the combination of cheesy toast and research must have knocked me out.

Buzzing again. I scrabble around until I find my phone. It's a text from Saanvi to Holden and me, and there's a video attached.

SAANVI: Oooooof! Look!

The video shows Ana sitting alone in the art room at The Mitch. She's picking her nose. As in, really going for it. I would almost say "excavating" rather than "picking."

ME: That's disgusting.

21

SAANVI: Our computer graphics group met this afternoon, and someone got the text and showed it to Ana. She FREAKED OUT! She ran out of the room. What should I do???

HOLDEN: Maybe stop sending the vid to other people?

SAANVI: I ONLY SENT IT TO YOU TWO!

ME: Ignore him. He's kidding. Poor Ana.

SAANVI: I know! I feel icky-fied.

HOLDEN: Have you texted her?

SAANVI: What do I say? I'm super losing it here.

HOLDEN: Say that everyone nose-picks. Who cares?

ME: Everyone does NOT nose-pick.

HOLDEN: Liar.

SANNVI: GUYS! SERIOUSLY NOT HELPFUL!

ME: How did someone get a video of this? How did she not notice?

SAANVI: Ikr? ☹

ME: Ask Ana if she needs to talk. So she doesn't feel alone in the world.

SAANVI: k. I'll try. Ty.

HOLDEN: Then offer her a tissue.

SAANVI: AAAARGH!

ME: So thoughtful.

HOLDEN: 😇

I grab my sketchpad again and start drawing Saanvi and Holden as I imagine them right now, holding their phones. Saanvi will be sitting cross-legged on her bed, one hand tugging at her hair. Holden will be sprawled on his couch, lit only by the glow of his phone screen and his TV.

The three of us met in an after-school art class in fourth grade, where we bonded over a mutual respect for micro-art painted onto grains of rice. We wanted to try it. Our teacher, unfortunately, wanted us to copy van Gogh's sunflowers. As in, she really, really wanted us to stay on topic. It's possible that Saanvi may have led a teensy class rebellion, with Holden (loudly) and me (silently) cheering her on.

Our teacher quit. They had to get a substitute for the rest of the term, and the substitute let us paint on basically whatever we wanted. (Incidentally, creating anything on a grain of rice is *completely* impossible.)

Back then, we all went to different elementary schools. When we found each other at the sixth-grade orientation to The Mitch, it was as if we'd rediscovered our lost soul mates. I was so nervous that day, I was practically shaking. But Saanvi turned her saucer-sized eyes to me, I smiled as I recognized her, and we spent the entire tour with our arms linked. At first, Holden slouched nearby, muttering jokes under his breath. But somehow, by the end of the tour, he was linked between us.

This was around the time Holden abandoned his acting and after-school activity schedule for his gaming obsession, and before Saanvi devoted all her spare hours to calculus and app development. But even though the two of them are getting more eccentric every year, they're still my favorites.

Mom arrives home, interrupting my doodling. She kicks off her shoes in the hallway, drops her sweater on the back of the living room chair, and smiles.

"I'm just here to shower and change. I brought leftovers."

She kisses my forehead and sets a giant takeout box on the coffee table.

Because Mom's a caterer, the word *leftovers* doesn't mean meatloaf. It means flaky mini pastries dolloped with fig compote, or cucumber rounds topped with spot prawns and mango chutney. It takes me about a millisecond to flip open the box and pop a tart into my mouth. Chocolate ganache. For a minute, it makes the whole world glow. These things could seriously solve world crises. Mom should serve them at national security conferences. She could give them to people on opposite sides of the drone security/privacy issue, and everyone would immediately compromise.

I think I'm audibly groaning.

"They're good, aren't they? Linda thought they'd be too rich, but I told her there's no such thing." She grins.

Mom and Linda started their company together when I was two, only a year after my dad died. Mom once told me she needed to rebuild her life, and she chose to focus on me and on her cooking. Now she creates the recipes while Linda organizes their events. The two of them are polar opposites, which makes for a lot of bickering. But, as George says, that's what keeps the company afloat. If Mom ran it alone, it would be all *beurre blanc* and no bookkeeping.

I move from sweet to savory and choose a chicken satay. Amazing how everything tastes better on a stick.

My phone buzzes.

SAANVI: No word from Ana.

ME: Want to come over? Mom made chocolate ganache tarts.

SAANVI: OMG. COMING OVER IMMEDIATELY.

Mom's already in the shower, so I yell through the bathroom door.

"Saanvi's on her way, okay?"

"Of course! Give her some tarts!" she calls back.

"Good idea."

When I open the door a few minutes later, I find both Saanvi and Holden on the threshold.

"He texted at seriously the exact moment I was leaving," Saanvi says. "I think he somehow knew about the tarts."

Holden shrugs. "Your mom's tarts and I have a psychic connection. We're like twins separated at birth."

Mom arrives at the door just in time to hear those words.

"You're the sweetest," she says, giving Holden a loud kiss on the cheek.

He actually blushes.

Mom's wearing a black dress that I bought for the school's winter dance last year. It looks way better (plus shorter and tighter) on her than it did on me, which is cosmically unfair.

"Sure, you can borrow it," I say.

"Thanks, sweetheart. I have to hurry to meet Frank. Don't stay up too late, okay?"

"You neither."

"No promises." She winks at us and she's out the door.

A millisecond later, she's back. "Forgot my purse!"

She hurries through the kitchen, into her bedroom, and back again. "Can't find it!"

Saanvi and I scour the area to help.

"What does it look like?" Saanvi asks.

"Little black handbag with a sparkly strap."

Eventually, I spot it on the kitchen counter, wedged between the wall and a stack of unopened mail.

"You're an angel," Mom says. "Got to go!"

And she's off, for good this time.

"You have the ultra-coolest mom ever," Saanvi says.

I stare at her.

"What? Everyone loses things sometimes."

"She loses everything, all the time! You should hear how often she lost *me*, when I was a kid."

Saanvi laughs as if I'm joking, throws herself onto the couch, and surveys the leftover treats. She goes straight for the chocolate, as does Holden. I drop to the floor beside them and choose a scallop on a square of puff pastry, tiny curlicues of lemon rind decorating the top.

"There's the family you get, and the family you choose," I say.

Saanvi grins. That's the slogan from a set of dollar-store mugs she bought us for Christmas last year. I still have mine.

I tangle my ankles between those of Holden and Saanvi and sigh happily. My life may not be perfect, but at least I'm not Ana.

On Tuesday morning, I drag myself out of bed and survey the wreckage. Couch cushions lie scattered around the room where they landed during our purse-search. There are chocolate-smeared paper doilies, broken skewers, and used forks spread like tsunami debris across the coffee table.

I groan. I can't believe I didn't clean up before I went to sleep. I must have been in some sort of sugar stupor.

Mom has added to the mess by leaving her purse and shoes strewn in the middle of the entranceway. Her dress—my dress!—lies in a rumpled heap in the bathroom.

I'm definitely not leaving the house in this state. But by the time I have the coffee table cleared and Mom's detritus organized, I'm almost late. Again! I throw on my uniform, string my ID around my neck, and grab a granola bar before rushing to the elevator.

"Good morning, Lou!" I call as I collect Holden and scoot past.

"Dangerous world out there," he says.

We pick up Saanvi and make it to the school gates just in time.

Ana's climbing the front steps ahead of us. It may be my imagination, but her pink barrette seems a little askew.

"Hi, Ana," Saanvi calls.

She turns bright red.

"Alizarin crimson," Holden whispers.

George gave us a collection of fancy color wheels a couple years ago, left over from an exhibit. Holden has always liked the names more than the actual colors.

"I'd call it quinacridone magenta," I say.

"GUYS, SHUT UP," Saanvi whisper-hisses.

It doesn't matter anyway. Ana's already pushed open the double doors.

We're only halfway up the stairs when it starts. We hear a symphony of whistles, catcalls, and hollers. A few slow claps. I pick out the voices of Josh, Max, and the other resident hooligans, who sound as if they're yelling from the stands of a soccer game.

The double doors bang open and Ana appears again, as if she's been spit out by the building itself. The noise dampens behind her as the doors swing shut.

"Whoa," Holden manages.

Saanvi and I both rush to provide moral support, but Ana dodges us. Before we can say anything, she scurries down the stairs and toward the street.

"That was intense," Holden mutters.

"HOLDEN!" Saanvi turns on him.

"What? What did I do?"

"Nothing! That's the entire point!"

She whips open the doors and disappears inside. I look back and forth between the school and the still sputtering Holden. Then the warning bell rings and I quickly follow her, flashing my ID card at the scanner as I pass through the lobby.

My phone buzzes almost immediately.

GEORGE: Glad you got there safely.

ME: I always get here safely. You don't need to check on me. :)

GEORGE: It makes me feel better when I get that little "ding" from the school system.

ME: Here I am. Dinging right along.

GEORGE: Have a lovely day, darling.

ME: ♥

I slide into my homeroom desk just as the second bell rings. Saanvi and Holden are still sniping at one another.

"There was nothing we could do," Holden whispers.

Which is true. If you pick your nose in public, what do you expect?

CHAPTER FOUR
LUNCH SPECIAL

WHEN I CAN'T find Holden or Saanvi at lunch hour, I wander into the cafeteria by myself. I collect a lunch special—a bowl of chili and a cheese bun, today—and then sit at our usual table against the bank of tall, leaded windows. The breeze seems to blow right through the glass, but we're farthest from the lunchroom supervisor and farthest from the stinky compost bins. Usually, we get the table to ourselves.

Not today.

Before I've had a single bite, Ana appears. Her eyes are even wider than usual and she's gripping her lunch tray so tightly that her tiny fingers are white.

At least she came back to school this morning. That was brave.

When she pauses at the end of my table, I reluctantly wave her toward a chair.

"Why are you by yourself?" she asks. "Where are Holden and Saanvi?"

Along with her school uniform, she's wearing pink-striped knee socks and a pink barrette with a bow on it. She'd look a little odd, even if she didn't have a copy of *The Miracle of Mitosis* balanced on the tray beside her chili.

"I heard about the video," I say.

If Saanvi were here, she'd probably kick me under the

30

table, but I figure I may as well bring things out in the open. Maybe Ana wants to talk about it. Besides, I didn't tell her I *saw* the video.

She pauses for a moment, then straightens her shoulders and gives me a slightly-too-bright smile. "Science test tomorrow," she says. "Do you want to quiz me? Do you have the same test this week? We could quiz each other?"

I don't have the same test, actually, because I don't have the same science teacher, but none of this seems to matter. She holds out her notes, shaking them a little when I don't grab them right away.

I'm saved from quiz practice only by a shadow that falls across our table. I look up to see Max Lin. As usual, he has an old-fashioned camera strung around his neck—the one thing that sets him apart from Josh and the other orangutans. Today, he's also carrying a plate of cafeteria cheesecake. He's draped a strip of white paper towel across his other arm.

Max places the cake in front of me with a flourish, as if he's Pierre at La Patisserie. He's obviously lost. Or he's lost his mind. Where are his sweaty, obnoxious friends? They always seem to travel in a pack.

"What's up, Max?"

"Happy Tuesday," he says.

Great. My friends leave me alone for one lunch hour, and I find myself in an asylum.

Max leans close to my ear. "Listen, I'm sorry, okay?"

Before I can ask what that's supposed to mean, he walks away.

I'm still staring after him when Holden and Saanvi set their trays on the table and sit down.

"Oh, good," Ana says. "Do you guys have the science test tomorrow? We were going to do an impromptu study session?"

"What's with the cake?" Holden asks.

"Was that Max?" Saanvi asks at the same time.

"He said it's because he's sorry," I tell her, shrugging.

Ignoring Ana's attempts to pass them flashcards (seriously, flashcards), they both dig their forks into the dessert.

"It could be poisoned," I warn.

"Do you think he likes you?" Saanvi asks.

"That's crazy."

"He probably lost a bet," Holden says.

Saanvi tosses a crust of her bun at him, but misses. Then I have to duck as someone from the next table looks around, wondering why it's raining cheese buns. When I poke my head up again, Holden's holding out a forkful of cake.

I have no idea how lunch hour got so surreal, but the cake is surprisingly good.

It's mostly gone when Ana brandishes her flashcards again.

"Bathroom break," Holden announces, leaving us.

"Poor guy," Ana says.

"What? Why?" Saanvi asks.

"He's so shy. The minute anyone suggests an activity, he leaves."

Saanvi snorts.

"He's not shy. He hates joining things," I explain.

Ana's eyes go even wider than usual. "But why?"

"Overscheduled childhood," I say.

"It's kind of like a hunger strike, except he refuses activities instead of food," Saanvi adds.

Ana looks completely confused, but the bell rings before she can ask more questions. And apparently she doesn't spend too long worrying about the issue. Halfway to home-room, Saanvi shows me a PixSnappy post on her phone.

"Cheesecake Deliciousness!!"

You've been tagged in a PixSnappy post by @AnaBananasBrain. Join PixSnappy now and see what your friends are up to.

Respond Now

Unsubscribe I Help

You are receiving invitation reminders from PixSnappy. We use your email address to make suggestions to our users in fun features like Connect with Friends.

Holden, Saanvi, and I have a study block together after lunch. We should probably work on our math while our genius friend Saanvi is available to help. But Holden's glued to his phone.

"Are you still checking the forums?" The forums are part of the school website, open to students only. It's where we post group assignments or ask each other homework questions.

"There's a whole string of embarrassing videos on here. Ana isn't the only one."

"Really?" Saanvi says.

We lean over so we can see his screen.

"Ack. Poor Marcus," I say. In the video, a flap of his shirt is sticking out of his wide-open fly.

"Why doesn't he get this taken down?" Holden asks.

"Maybe he doesn't realize," I say.

Saanvi wrinkles her nose. "A few extra people laughing at Marcus wouldn't be a ginormous change."

Which is sadly true. Marcus Arnit is greeted with chants of "Armpit! Armpit! Armpit!" on a regular basis. It's not likely his social life could get worse.

"And who's going to tell Ms. Crofton she shouldn't sit like that?" Saanvi adds.

I lean over again to see a photo of our art teacher perched atop her desk with her legs crossed. Ms. Crofton has an entire collection of ethically produced bamboo dresses. They're fairly clingy, and this one obviously slid up when she sat on her desk. There's a substantial amount of thigh showing.

"Can you log out?" I beg Holden. "Looking at this makes me feel gross."

"True," Saanvi says. "Plus . . . we have super-fun algebra to do!" She grins at us, semi-evilly and semi-hopefully.

"There's something weird here," Holden says, ignoring her. "Marcus's video is taken from a strange angle. And Ana's not in the middle of the shot, either. Who do you think took these?"

I reach over. "Let me look."

"Or, we could leave Ana alone and think about order of operations," Saanvi says.

When I hold up a finger to pause her, she groans.

I stare at Holden's phone. And maybe it's because of Ms. Sutton looking at the camera in our ethics class, or maybe it's because I was staring at that photo of Banksy's words written directly beneath the security cameras, but I suddenly know exactly where these shots came from.

"Hey, guys? No one *took* these videos. Someone *stole* them," I say.

"What?"

They give me matching confused looks.

"These are from the school security system. Look at Marcus's. It's taken from the corner of the humanities room."

I'm not a math guru like Saanvi, or a child star like Holden, but I'm good at turning puzzle pieces in my mind and seeing which way they click together. My brain is always drawing maps and measuring angles, whether or not I want it to.

There's only one way these video angles make sense.

"You're right," Holden mutters, taking his phone back.

"How did someone get into the security system?" Saanvi asks. "It should be encrypted."

"Good question."

"You're the computer genius." Holden raises his eyebrows at Saanvi. It's clearly a challenge, and she never turns down a challenge.

Order of operations is forgotten. She tugs her laptop from her bag. For the rest of our study period, she sits hunched over the screen, muttering to herself. Holden and I are left to do our math homework on our own. As it turns out, I'm much better at order of operations than he is. Math isn't my favorite subject, but it *is* about puzzles, in a different form.

Saanvi barely says a word for the rest of the day. I text her after dinner, to see if she's made progress.

ME: Any luck?

> **SAANVI:** Still trying.

> **ME:** How can you see who's accessed the system, anyway?

> **SAANVI:** Complicated. Show you tmrw.

> **ME:** Nvm. That's your department.

I stay up too late watching TV, then working for a while on my Banksy project, then drawing possible portraits of what Banksy might look like. Finally, I flop into bed and tell myself to sleep.

Mom's still not home.

When I click the Find Friends app on my phone, I can see her tiny picture, hovering over a house ten minutes away. She's catering a private dinner party tonight. I watch for a few minutes to see if she'll start moving toward me. But no.

I'm used to her being out. It's not like I can't stay on my own. But some nights, our apartment seems too quiet.

I used to have nightmares when I was little, after a boy from our neighborhood was kidnapped. (Really. I still have a poster around here somewhere. *Missing: Daniel Donavan*. It turned out his dad took him, and it was some sort of custody dispute, but still. Scary.)

Tonight, Mom appears to have been kidnapped by work. Again. Her little picture continues to hover, ten minutes away.

My phone buzzes, making me jump.

HOLDEN: What if you had brain-freeze, a foot cramp, and hit your funny bone all at the same time?

ME: And stubbed your toe?

HOLDEN: Whoa.

ME: You might spontaneously combust.

HOLDEN: Can you try? I'll get it on video. I'll be rich.

ME: You're already rich.

HOLDEN: But think of the fame. The glory. The PixSnappy followers.

ME: Go to sleep.

HOLDEN: Your mom home tonight?

ME: Not yet. Soon.

HOLDEN: Well, pretend Saanvi and I are there for one of our epic food fests.

ME: With s'mores hot chocolate.

ME: Sweet dreams.

I try to sleep for a while. Half an hour later, I give up, flick on my lamp, and grab George's book from the floor beside my bed.

I looked up *subversive* earlier today. It means: "intended to undermine an existing system." Basically, it's a fancy word for being a rebel.

I am entirely, officially in love with this artist.

On the book's cover, there's a painting of a drab-looking man, a worker of some sort. He carries a couple rolls of paper, along with a bucket and paintbrush. Beside him on the wall it says FOLLOW YOUR DREAMS in black and white. And there's a big red banner overtop that reads CANCELLED.

Banksy started painting when he was part of a crew of graffiti artists in Bristol, England. (I guess all those other crew members must know who he is, but they're not telling!) Now he works all over the world—in New York City, on the wall between Israel and Palestine, in Paris, even at Disneyland. He uses stencils to help him paint more quickly on walls and buildings.

I flip to a print of silhouettes—women, children, and old people. They're all running from a man in a suit, but he's not holding a weapon. He's holding a red graph line, the kind that shows the stock market going up. I think the picture is saying that people making money are chasing or punishing or stealing from people without money. It's kind of awesome. (The painting, not the punishing and stealing.)

As I stare at the pages, my insides start to split apart. Half of me desperately wants to be a real, serious artist one day. The type of person who has her own gallery openings. Someone with a studio in an old brick building, where huge windows let the sun stream onto my easel and spill across the dozen canvases spread around the room.

The other half of me looks at Banksy's works and knows I'm never going to be half as good. How does he manage to put so much emotion into pictures done with spray paint, and only one or two colors?

Rattle.

I hear Mom's keys in the lock, and then the telltale triple-drop of her shoes and purse on the floor. Quickly, I click off my lamp and slide the Banksy book onto my rug. I don't want Mom to worry, or to think I've been waiting for her. Besides, I should be able to sleep now.

Maybe I'll dream in stencils.

CHAPTER FIVE
THE QUICK FLIP

ON WEDNESDAY MORNING, I step out of the elevator to find both Saanvi and Holden waiting in my lobby.

I know immediately that something's wrong. Holden's eyebrows almost meet in the middle, and Saanvi's biting her lip. I feel as if I should brace myself.

There's not much to hold on to in the marble expanse of the lobby.

"Dangerous world out there," Lou says.

No one answers.

I follow my friends outside. "What's going on?"

Holden shrugs, and neither of them say anything until we're around the corner. Then they drop onto a bus stop bench and tug me down between them.

"*What* is going on?"

Saanvi passes me her phone, and I press Play.

Crap.

Crap, crap, and triple crap.

This is worse than nose-picking. Much, much worse.

Welcome to the Mitchell Academy forums.
This is a place for students to learn new information and help their peers. Please follow all forum rules and guidelines in order to create an atmosphere of respect.

Mitch Girl Gone Wild posted by admin28x5
on April 24th at 1:10 AM

Miranda88: This is mean. You should take this down.
Plantster: Way to take a joke, Miranda.
EVF: Not like it didn't happen. The TRUTH WILL OUT!
MTG3456XXX: Take it off, baby!

The film is shot from above and slightly behind me. I'm sitting alone in the library, crowded bookshelves framing me. Music swells—ridiculous music, as if someone clicked the "suspense" theme in a filmmaking app. I glance first over one shoulder, then the other.

The video flips to slow motion. As if I'm doing a secret striptease, I reach down and pull at the hem of my shirt. The fabric slides up slowly, exposing my bra strap, then my shoulders. With a final flick, I peel it off entirely.

The video cuts to black.

I can't look up. Holden and Saanvi huddle close on either side of me on the bus stop bench, but I can't look at them.

When I try to make words, nothing comes out. I feel as if someone's punched me.

"Dom . . . ," Saanvi says eventually. "Why were you stripping in the library?"

"She was *not* stripping," Holden says, and I'm so grateful, I lean into him.

I was *not* stripping. I'm probably the person least likely to take off my clothes at school. Most likely to kiss a boy: Miranda Bowen. Most likely to seek attention: Ana Kavanaugh. And not even those two would strip on camera. Josh and Max would do it, but they'd do almost anything, and they wouldn't care about video evidence.

"But why?" Saanvi asks again.

"I didn't!" I blurt. "My shirt was inside out, and I flipped it. There was no one else there!"

As the last word dissolves into a wail, Holden wraps an arm around my shoulders.

Over the past three years, we've had a half-dozen school talks about social media safety. They've all focused on one thing: you shouldn't put your breasts on the internet. You shouldn't text them to your boyfriend. You shouldn't let anyone take pictures of them. You shouldn't put them on PixSnappy. Various speakers repeated this until I wanted to grab the microphone and tell them to move on, because *of course* no one would ever go topless on the internet.

Except now I've done exactly that.

I feel sick.

I drop my head into my hands, staring at the pavement and wishing I could disappear into it. "It was a few days ago, before Ana's video. I didn't even remember doing it until now."

"You forgot about the cameras," Saanvi says.

"I'm so sick of those cameras," Holden growls.

"Who sent the file? Where did it come from?" I ask.

Saanvi takes back her phone. She scrolls to the menu labeled "Shotz" and hands the screen to me.

Mine is the third entry. Ana's nose-picking video has disappeared, so I come right after Marcus Arnit's gaping fly.

"This is horrible. Who's posting these?"

Saanvi shakes her head.

"Someone with the skills to hack the system," Holden says. "Or a few people. These are all different usernames."

"I found a list of everyone who's accessed the site, and a list of student and usernames, but they don't match any of these posts," Saanvi says. "I need administrator access to figure out more."

"People wouldn't post these with their own names," I say.

"Do you think a stranger could have access?" Holden asks.

"Great. Russian hackers have seen my side-boob, along with the entire student population of The Mitch."

"You can't see your . . . you know," Holden says. If I weren't in the midst of a personal crisis, I'd say he was blushing manganese violet.

"It's basically just your bra," Saanvi says.

"I DON'T WANT MY BRA ON THE INTERNET!"

A woman walking her dog turns to stare at us, and I flush my own shade of violet.

I groan. "How did this happen to me?"

"Maybe no one hacked the system," Saanvi says. "Maybe someone stole the passwords."

"Like who?" Holden says.

"Josh?" I suggest.

Along with being the biggest jerk at The Mitch, Josh is Principal Plante's son.

Saanvi looks back and forth between us. Holden shrugs.

My stomach sinks as I remember the cafeteria yesterday. "Hey, when Max dropped off that cheesecake and he said sorry . . . do you think he was talking about this?"

"That'd be weird," Holden says.

"I know."

All of this is weird.

"Plus, Max isn't smart enough," he says.

"We're going to be late," Saanvi tells us.

"So what?" Holden says.

"Dom hates being late."

"Today might be an exception."

They talk back and forth over my head.

I force myself to suck in a giant breath. I have to get it together. It feels like trying to shore up a crumbling sandcastle— not entirely effective. But another breath, and another, and I think it might be possible. So people have now seen my bra. Big deal, right? It's just a bra.

"I'll take her to my house," Holden says. "No one's home today."

"The school will call her mom."

"The school *is* going to call my mom. My mom's going to tell George. And they're both going to look at a video of me stripping on the internet." I would like to be sucked up by a black hole. Disappeared by the universe. Now would be good.

"They're not going to call your mom. None of the teachers pay attention to the forums. Do you think the art teacher's skirt would still be posted if Principal Plante was paying attention?"

Saanvi has a point.

"So . . . school?" Holden says.

"She's going to have to face it sometime." Saanvi nods.

"Stop talking about me like I'm not here."

I drop my head between my knees. Saanvi leans down so she can see my face.

"Do you want to go home, or do you want to go to school?"

I have no idea. I can't think.

When the first camera appeared, high on our cafeteria wall, Holden and I bickered about it. He called it "a Big Brother surveillance tool" and "a symbol of the corporate overlords," which didn't really make sense. The school was a nonprofit organization, not a corporation, I told him. And even if it *were* a corporation, it's not like anyone cared what we did, as long as we went to class and acted like normal human beings.

"There are scary things happening," I'd said. "What about school shootings?"

"How are cameras going to stop a shooting?"

"At least it's something! Kids might feel safer with the cameras here."

"You have serious anxiety issues AND you've been brainwashed."

He practically yelled it, then he stomped out of the cafeteria, and I couldn't do anything except sit there with my mouth open.

When Saanvi appeared a little while later, I pretended everything was fine. Then we saw Holden in class after lunch, and he pretended everything was fine. And that was sort of the end of it. Until now.

Do I want to go home, wait for Mom to wake up, and tell

her I got shirtless on camera? Or do I want to go to school and see what Josh has to say about my bra?

Wow. Those are stellar choices.

"Either way, we've got this," Holden says. Which is actually comforting.

"Everyone has boobs," Saanvi says.

"Not everyone," Holden objects.

"Man boobs."

"Not helping!" I tell them.

Though strangely, it is sort of helping.

Everyone has boobs, and mine were mostly covered up. A bra is an everyday item of clothing. Holden and Saanvi will stick by me. I'm going to have to go to school sometime. Unless I'm planning to quit The Mitch, I might as well get this over with.

"Okay, let's go."

"Are you sure?" Saanvi asks.

"Of course I'm not sure. But I want to go to ethics, anyway. Our project summaries are due."

Banksy. That's how I'll spend the morning. I'll think only about Banksy.

"Ms. Sutton will let you—" Holden says.

"If Josh and Max are going to—" Saanvi says, at the same time.

"What side are you on? I thought you wanted me to go?"

"You're right," Saanvi says quickly. Then she smirks. "And if Josh did this, and I can prove it, he's going to be very, very sorry."

Even though I feel as if a passing city bus has run me over, leaving me entirely two-dimensional, I can't help smiling a little as she pops a fist into her palm. Saanvi weighs about as much as a stick, but she might actually follow through on that threat. She never backs down from a fight.

Though I don't quite see how she's going to fight something that's been anonymously posted online.

This is going to be gruesome.

We're off the bench now and heading for school. I have to force my legs to take each new step. Ethics, then math, then lunch. I can do this.

"All right. Get moving. We're going to be late," I say, mostly to myself.

My video is probably the hit entertainment option in the hallways this morning. *Everyone* will be watching it. My throat begins to close.

Banksy. Best to think only about Banksy.

Holden reaches into his pocket and hands me a wad of tissue.

I look at it suspiciously.

"It's clean!" he insists. "It's just squished from my pocket."

Reluctantly, I dab under my eyes. It's a good thing I don't wear Mom-level mascara.

The bell has already rung, so we have to check in with Ms. Marcie, the office secretary. She has tight dyed-blonde curls and a permanent smile, even when she's clicking her tongue at our lateness. She passes us three yellow late slips.

"Hurry and get to class, before Ms. Plante sees you," she whispers.

Exactly. We'll hurry and get to class, and I'll think about Banksy, and everything will be fine.

Banksy has a thing for rats. He paints rats dressed like people, rats holding protest placards, rats climbing around

"No Climbing" signs, rats playing ball beneath "No Playing" signs. He likes rats.

I'll think about Banksy.

I'm going to pretend this never happened. And I'm convinced my plan has potential. At least until Holden and I arrive at ethics and learn that no one else is going to let me forget.

CHAPTER SIX
THE AFTERMATH

THE CLASSROOM is humming with murmured conversations and keyboard tapping until we walk through the door.

Everyone falls silent. Their eyes go wide. Their heads swivel toward me. One guy's standing in the aisle with a handful of sharpened pencils, which hit the floor in a clattering avalanche. He flushes to match his freckles.

"Venetian red with a dab of chrome yellow," Holden mutters.

I pick my way to the front, deliver my late slip, and slide into my desk.

Max is kneeling on the floor now, camera raised, framing a shot of the pencil avalanche. Behind me, Josh and the rest of the eighth-grade boy gang squawk and cackle like a flock of garbage-eating seagulls. When I glance back, Josh smirks at me.

A wave of pure rage arrives, which actually helps with the humiliation factor. My hands shake as I open my binder and rifle through the papers for my Banksy proposal.

Project Proposal
Banksy's Street Art
Dominica Rivers

Banksy is an anonymous street artist. He began as a graffiti painter with the DryBreadZ crew in Bristol,

England, in the early 1990s. He has a recognizable style using stencils and slogans. A lot of Banksy's work comments on current events or political themes. For example, in 2015 he painted a migrant camp in France with Apple cofounder Steve Jobs standing in the middle of it, holding a Macintosh computer. (Steve Jobs was the son of a Syrian immigrant.)

Banksy inspires me because of the messages in his art, because of the bravery it must take to create his work, and because he creates art for its meaning rather than for personal fame. These are the themes I will be exploring in my project.

Behind me, they all have their phones out. There's a long, low whistle.

"What exactly is going on in here today?" Ms. Sutton says. "Back to work, everyone."

"Ignore them," Holden whispers.

"Done," I say, between clenched teeth. I take out a black pen to underline my project heading. Too hard. I rip the paper.

A high five echoes through the room.

I make the mistake of squeezing my eyes closed for a moment, and the whole video replays on the backs of my eyelids. The horrible music. The slow motion. The way I grab the bottom of my shirt and then tug, wiggle, tug until it slides over my head . . .

Another burst of laughter. "Dominica," Josh whispers. "Have you considered doing this professionally?"

"Of course she has. This is all practice," someone says.

I'm frozen in my desk, like a squirrel in the middle of the road, staring as a truck looms closer and closer.

"Boys!" Ms. Sutton calls. "Focus, please!"

My eyes go blurry with tears.

I can't do this. I stand and turn toward the door. My hip catches the corner of my desk, and my binder crashes to the floor. A few papers flutter out. I can't stop to collect them.

"Dominica Rivers, where are you going?" Ms. Sutton sounds entirely confused by the world this morning.

"She's not feeling well," Holden tells her.

"Dominica, you can—"

I don't hear the rest of her words. I'm already bolting down the hall to the nearest bathroom. I barely make it to the toilet before I lose my breakfast. My hands are shaking again. My whole body's shaking.

Also, there's nothing good about having my face this close to a school toilet.

I sit back against the cubical wall, trying to slow my breathing. I'm still clutching my pen, so tightly that my nails are digging into my palm. I force myself to loosen my fingers.

I might have to homeschool. Convert to Catholicism and transfer to Our Lady of Mercy? I don't know if I can survive here.

On the cubicle wall in front of me, someone's scribbled *Rebecca is a skank*. Who's Rebecca? And what did she do to deserve this? I bet she hasn't flashed her bra on camera. What are they going to say about *me* on these cubicle walls?

My pen's in motion before I've stopped to think words like *graffiti* or *vandalism*. At first, I'm turning the letters of *skank* into a rat, the kind of rat Banksy draws. But the tall *k* at the end morphs into a bushy tail, and my drawing winds up being a squirrel with wide eyes and a whiskery nose. A squirrel trying to figure out exactly how it got itself in the middle of a road, blinded by headlights.

I run lines of black ink over and over one another until the word beneath entirely disappears.

There. I've done something for Rebecca, at least.

As I'm wondering where I should go from this bathroom floor—because I am absolutely *not* going back to ethics right now—the door squeaks open.

"It's just me."

Miranda's voice. I can see her heels (leopard-print today) from under the door.

"Ms. Sutton asked me to check if you're okay."

I reach to push open the cubicle. Miranda passes me a handful of paper towel, which is nice of her. She knows exactly what's happened, because of course she's seen the video.

"Anything I can do?"

This is an excellent question. Is there anything anyone can do about this?

"Can you get Saanvi for me? I think she's in math."

"Done."

For a journalist, Miranda asks surprisingly few questions. I'm grateful for that. As she disappears out the bathroom door, I decide I might even forgive her for the head-massage incident.

She must jog all the way to the math classroom. Impossibly quickly, Saanvi's sitting on the floor beside me.

Miranda gives us a brief wave from the door. "I'll tell Ms. Sutton you're resting."

She's gone before I can thank her.

Saanvi slides closer to me on the tile floor, presses her shoulder against mine, and waits.

"Only a really good friend would sit on these tiles. You're probably absorbing more *E. coli* every second," I say eventually.

"True."

A horrible thought strikes me. "What if kids go home and show the forum post to their parents?"

Parents don't use the forums, but that doesn't mean they won't see the post.

"No one's going to do that."

"How do you know? Someone will tell, then their parents will call my mom, and then George will see the video, and then . . ."

"No one's going to tell! Have you seen Ana's mom in the office, complaining about Ana's video? No. Everyone got over the nose-picking in less than twenty-four hours. This will be the same."

It's tempting to believe her. But there's no way Saanvi can keep the video from popping up again, at any time, or guarantee my mom won't see it.

I sigh and tilt my head back against the cubicle wall. "Maybe I can switch schools."

"Absolutely not. You're stronger than that. Besides, you can't leave me."

"You didn't hear how those guys in the back row were acting."

"What were they doing?"

When I don't answer right away, she nudges my ribs. "Let's give them all the wrong answers to the next math test."

I shake my head.

"Frame them for plagiarism? Dye their basketball uniforms pink?"

"They're kind of ruining my life," I tell her. "I don't think pink uniforms are the answer."

She falls silent but she doesn't move away, which I appreciate. It's possible the warmth of her shoulder is the only thing keeping me upright.

"This is too big for us," I say finally. "We need to tell someone."

"Who? Your mom?"

The idea makes me want to throw up again. I won't be able to handle the look of disappointment on her face. Or George's appalled expression.

"I could call my dad?" Saanvi offers.

Which is incredibly nice of her, but the first thing Mr. Agarwal will do is tell my mom. Then they'll both call Ms. Plante.

I try to shove down all my anger and embarrassment and think clearly.

"I need the video deleted," I say. "That's the first step. And we can't let people get away with posting this sort of thing. The school—"

"You want to talk to Ms. Plante?"

"No. But yes."

"Alright. Let's go, then." She doesn't even seem to consider sending me alone.

I'm having the worst possible day. But at least I have the best possible friends.

The whole way from the bathroom to the office, I see only cameras. Were there always this many? There's a black globe at every corner of the hallway, and above every exit door. I feel as if I have one of Holden's video game maps in my mind, with little red dots popping up as I plot the security.

There are two above the office door. I squint at them. One seems to point out toward the foyer, the other down at the counter.

"What do you need, girls?"

I'm so focused on the cameras, I barely hear Ms. Marcie.

Saanvi answers, and Ms. Marcie ushers us toward the principal's door.

I stub my toe on the corner, but I barely feel it.

Saanvi links her arm through mine. Probably to make sure I don't stagger for the bathroom again. I feel more green than ever.

Oxide of chromium, Holden would say.

When Principal Plante sees us in her doorway, she leans forward, folds her hands together, and smiles a tight, tooth-baring smile. Or maybe that last part is my imagination.

"What can I do for you girls?"

She's wearing the type of wide, red-striped scarf you see on flight attendants. If this were one of the Rick Riordan novels that Saanvi and I used to devour, our principal would turn into a Greek monster any moment now.

In reality, she's some sort of organizational expert. Which, when I think about it, might be closely related to Greek monster-dom.

My brain is going haywire. I think it's trying to escape this room.

We perch on the two black chairs facing Ms. Plante's desk. I look to Saanvi, then back to the principal. I take a deep breath.

"We have an issue with the forums," I say. And then . . . nothing.

Saanvi plunges ahead. "Someone posted a video of Dom.

55

It makes it look like she's doing something she would never, ever do."

Except that I did.

"I see," Ms. Plante says. Except that she doesn't. "Let's have a look at this video of yours."

After two tries, I manage to tap in my security code and hand over my phone.

Ms. Plante presses Play, waits until the end, and then watches the video a second time. It takes approximately a century, while my stomach roils like the inside of a washing machine.

I concentrate on breathing.

Does a gorgon have multiple heads, or is that a hydra? And which one turns you to stone?

When Ms. Plante finally looks up, there's a sharp crease between her carefully plucked eyebrows.

I don't know how some people manage to get in trouble over and over. I never want to be in this office again. And the video isn't even my fault.

She settles her glare on me.

Gorgon. It's definitely a gorgon that turns you to stone.

"Explain this please, Dominica. Why exactly were you taking your clothes off at school? Is this some sort of joke?"

I shake my head. "My shirt was on inside out. I flipped it around. There was no one in the library."

"Obviously *someone* was there." She spins the phone back toward me as if she doesn't want it contaminating her fingers any longer.

Saanvi looks as if she wants to kick Ms. Plante under the desk. "There was no one in the room, Ms. Plante. This is from the school security camera."

If our principal's face looked threatening before, it turns downright thunderous now.

"That's absurd."

I nudge the screen back toward her. "You can tell by the angle."

She slaps a hand on her desk, hard enough to make my phone rattle.

"This sort of behavior will not be tolerated."

For a nanosecond, I think she's talking about the behavior of the person who stole the footage. Then she points a finger at me.

"You. Keep your clothes on."

She shifts her finger toward Saanvi. "And you. I don't want to hear another word about this issue."

She stands and opens her door, dismissing us.

I grab my phone. There are so many questions I want to ask. Will Ms. Plante get the post deleted? How quickly? Who has access to the school security systems? How is she going to find out who did this? I want to know more. I want to know everything. But apparently the whole gorgon/stone thing is still happening. I stand frozen in front of her desk, looking between the principal and the door, my mouth opening and closing, and all that comes out, stuttered and quavering, is, "So . . . you'll . . . ?"

"I will deal with the situation."

There is absolutely no quaver in Ms. Plante's voice.

I escape past her scarf-bow and toward the foyer, clutching Saanvi's arm again.

We almost run smack into Max's mom. She's leaning against the receptionist's desk, her long fingernails tapping against her turquoise leather purse. Max's mom is the chair of the PAC, the parent advisory committee.

She smiles over us, toward the principal. "Good afternoon, Kathryn," she calls brightly. (Who knew the principal had a first name?)

I look back. Ms. Plante's eyebrows have melted into their regular positions.

"Patricia. What a nice surprise," she says.

She spares us one last glance.

"My door is always open, girls."

Then she ushers Max's mom inside and shuts it firmly behind her.

I don't go straight home after school. I'm still too mad and cringing and shaky. If Mom's home, I won't be able to pretend everything's okay. So I turn off a block from our building, slide past a "No Trespassing" sign, and slip through a gap in the orange construction fence.

I found this place years ago. There are crumbling concrete foundations where a mansion used to stand, and a sprawling overgrown garden along one side of the lot. Japanese maples arch over a small pond. If I stand near the water, fish dart into the shadows.

I asked Lou about it. He said the developers are having a fight with the city about how many apartments they can build on the site. I hope they don't settle their argument anytime soon.

Today, I stop abruptly a step or two into the garden. There's a family of raccoons playing in my spot by the pond.

A portly mama raccoon squats at the edge while three kits splash and tumble in the water. It looks like a Red Cross swimming lesson for wildlife. I sink to the grass and sit perfectly still, watching, until they clamber out, shake, and trundle off toward the shrubs.

I don't bother moving, even then. Birds call from the trees above me and leaves rustle in the breeze. I feel calmer sitting here on the grass between the wall and the water.

I close my eyes and let a map of the city unfurl in my mind. Most of the streets run in a grid pattern, but our neighborhood was designed by a master planner a century ago. Wide avenues curve along topographical lines, to make everything seem more exclusive. Sometimes, I picture my forgotten, park-like lot as if it's the eye of a storm, with the streets spiraling out around it.

I've momentarily escaped from the world. There are no cameras to duck, no videos to fear, no whispers to ignore. It's possible I should pitch a tent in this garden and refuse to leave.

CHAPTER SEVEN
THE TWO-LEGGED SPECIES

I CHECK as soon as I get home. The videos are gone. The entire forum string has disappeared.

It takes me a moment to absorb the news. I lean against the kitchen counter, letting the relief flow through me. I know this doesn't mean the situation is over, but at least it's not going to get worse.

Grabbing my laptop, I head for my room, telling myself to put the whole disaster behind me. I'll work on my project for ethics. Between the binder-dropping and the puking, I didn't hand in my proposal. Hopefully Ms. Sutton will accept it tomorrow. And hopefully she'll approve my subject choice.

The videos are gone.

I'm almost giddy as I settle on my bed with George's Banksy book and my computer.

Banksy may not be as famous as Rachel Carson or as vocal as Malala, but he's equally smart. And he really cares about things. Global things. Once, he repainted Monet's *Water Lilies*, except the pond water was polluted with a pylon and shopping carts.

My phone buzzes, jolting me back to reality.

HOLDEN: Hey, has Plante found out who did this?

ME: Doubt it.

ME: She hasn't called my mom yet. Think she's going to?

HOLDEN: Maybe doesn't want to admit her security system's not secure.

ME: Securitas genera victoria.

HOLDEN: So stupid.

HOLDEN: And Plante's a container of sour milk.

HOLDEN: Mixed with anchovies.

ME: A moldy scoop of cold corn casserole.

HOLDEN: A woodchuck with a skin condition.

ME: A mutant two-legged giraffe.

HOLDEN: Dude, all giraffes have two legs. Duh.

ME: What are you talking about?

HOLDEN: What are YOU talking about?

ME: Giraffes have four legs.

HOLDEN: Bahahahaha! Good one.

ME: ?

HOLDEN: 😄

ME: Um . . .

HOLDEN: Just google "two-legged giraffes" and count the legs. You'll see.

ME: Or you can google "giraffe" and count the legs.

HOLDEN: Listen, I should know. I've been to Australia.

ME: GIRAFFES ARE FROM AFRICA!

Only Holden could make me laugh after everything that's happened.

I pull my laptop closer, then spend a few minutes closing the pop-up ads about drones and art supplies. Eventually, I open a new file.

I stare at the blank screen, trying to think of a genius-level first line for my Banksy presentation to the class.

Nothing.

Which is probably because I'm not a genius. I mean, I'm

good at math. I'm a decent artist. But people like Saanvi and Ana are certified prodigies. Even Holden has his famous past. I'm more like the resident imposter.

I don't know how I got into this fancy school in the first place.

Well, I do, actually. It was George.

When I was in fifth grade, she hosted a gallery exhibition by a famous collage creator. Mom catered the opening night. I tagged along, but it was only exciting for the first ten minutes. After I'd stuffed myself with cheese-and-compote bites, I quickly got bored. The place was packed with women in long black dresses and men in suits, everyone drinking wine and saying serious things about color palettes, texture combinations, and the artist's incredible sense of line.

I wandered into George's office at the back of the gallery, a place where I'd been coloring and drawing for years. This time, because of the collages outside, I tore up some blank blue-and-green invoice forms on George's desk, creating tiny petal shapes and piecing them together on a sheet of printer paper. Tearing, tucking, taping into place. It was something to do.

The event went on for so long, I fell asleep with my cheek pressed to the paper. Mom came and pried me off the desk at some point, and took me home to bed. I completely forgot about my collage.

Apparently, it was a Fibonacci sequence. That's a pattern found in seashells, pinecones, and spiral galaxies, but not generally in children's collages. You take the two previous numbers and add them together to get the next. For example: 1, 1, 2, 3, 5, 8, 13 . . .

I don't know how George recognized it. My grandma knows a surprising amount about a surprising number of things. A few months later, she spirited me away to testing with a woman who had a fluffy white dog, beanbag chairs, and an entire office stuffed with puzzles. I scored in the ninety-ninth percentile for visual-spatial ability, but I didn't know that until later. I didn't know until George arrived at brunch one weekend with an acceptance letter to The Mitch.

She and Mom had a gigantic fight about it in our living room.

It was the only time I'd ever heard them openly argue. George insisted she'd pay my fees, and Mom yelled things like "financial independence" and "charity case" and "elitist private school." George countered with "potential" and "intellect."

My grandma won, obviously. But I've always been a little unhappy that Mom argued with her about the money, and not about the fact that George had submitted my collage without asking. Maybe my teachers think I have some amazing future in Fibonacci-inspired art, but all I was doing was copying the collage creator with the incredible sense of line.

It's likely that I'm a fake genius who's only good at puzzles.

Maybe that's why I'm drawn to Banksy. I'm not saying he's an imposter, obviously, but he's not trying to be some bigwig capital-A Artist, either. He's just a guy. No one even knows what he looks like.

I could handle a little anonymity in my life right now.

At school on Thursday morning, Saanvi and I are swept into the stream of students hurrying to first period. It feels surreal. I don't think I should be here. I should be somewhere far, far away. Antarctica, possibly.

Ana catches up to us, clutching *The Miracle of Mitosis* again. Or still.

"Everything okay?" she chirps.

Saanvi and I glance at one another. It's great that the forum posts have disappeared, but everything is definitely not okay. It shouldn't be okay for Ana, either. How did she go from nose-picking nightmare to miracle of mitosis so quickly?

"Fine," Saanvi and I say at the same time.

"You look a bit tired," Ana tells me.

Maybe she was the only person in the school who didn't see my video. She probably spent yesterday solving climate change or saving endangered penguins. Or she's already writing a memoir about her own social media mishap and how she bravely overcame it.

She bounces on the balls of her feet. "Dommi, I was think-ing we could have a study session, for our ethics project? Saanvi, you could come too, of course, if you want to hang out. We could all brainstorm together. And then we'll make sure our ideas don't overlap, too. We could go to my house..."

"We have a lot going on right now," I say, in what must be a world-record-breaking understatement.

"But you don't even know when—"

Josh whips past the three of us.

"Hey, Dom," he calls over his shoulder. "Looking good."

Which wouldn't be horrible if he didn't cup his hands to his chest as he said it.

Every time I think I might be okay, or that having had my bra appear on the forums isn't a major problem if viewed from space, something like this happens and I feel my insides crumble.

Saanvi immediately puts a hand on my arm. Ana stares after Josh, one miniature eyebrow raised. I can tell she's about to ask me what's going on, and I really don't want to explain. For once I'm almost glad when Mr. Nowak appears.

"Get a move on, girls!"

Before his voice stops echoing from the lockers, the three of us are hurrying up the stairs toward humanities. I have no binder, no paper, no pens, but Mr. Lee doesn't seem to notice. As soon as we arrive, he turns to the board and begins dron-ing on about the golden age of Roman poetry.

I put my fingers on my temples, as if that might stop my brain from disintegrating.

"What's up?" Holden mouths from across the aisle, but I shake my head.

From the desk behind mine, Saanvi keeps sympathetically patting my shoulder. Which is going to make me cry soon.

The back row, as always, is a chorus of rustlings and whispers.

I glance back and accidentally meet Max's gaze. I jerk my eyes forward again, but my ears stay tuned. The guys are listing numbers. I can't make any sense of them.

"Seriously? I could rack up a billion points before you even start." That's Josh's voice.

"I'd like to see you try."

"Start counting," Josh says.

"Ms. Rivers?" When Mr. Lee calls my name, I snap to attention. He waits, eyebrows raised.

"Uh . . . could you repeat the question, please?"

I hate that I blush so easily. I hate that I'm such a pleaser, humiliated when I miss one question. Josh could miss a thousand and he wouldn't care.

"Reasons for the eventual downfall of the Roman Empire," Mr. Lee repeats. He's tall and thin and wears a black suit to school every single day. According to the historical record, he last smiled in 1973.

"Um . . . assassinations?"

The back row erupts in snickers because that word contains *ass* and because they're morons.

Mr. Lee ignores them.

"That might be considered a symptom rather than a cause," he says. "Correct answers include invading tribes, government corruption, unsustainable expansion . . ."

Ana waves her hand in the air and says something about lead poisoning.

"An interesting point," Mr. Lee says.

I scowl. Behind me, the whispering continues. Then a crunched-up ball of paper lands on the floor beside my desk. When I lean down to get it, a long, slow wolf whistle sounds from behind me.

Saanvi spins around. "Will you guys shut up?"

Josh throws his hands in the air as if he's completely innocent and has never had a wrongful thought in his life.

"Idiot," I mutter.

Mr. Lee clicks his tongue.

"Temper, girls," he says.

Tears spring to my eyes. I swear, I have a disability. I wish I could amputate my tear ducts. Why is this happening to me?

I face resolutely forward, blink hard, and press my lips together.

I find myself staring at an empty desk. It's Marcus's spot, I realize, but there's no sign of him. I try to remember when I last saw him. Did he finally check the forums, and find the video of his shirt flapping from his open fly?

A random burst of laughter from the back row.

It's sort of serendipitous that Mr. Lee's talking about the end of the Roman Empire. I can think of a few empires I'd like to end today.

The day ticks by so slowly, I feel as if the universe is torturing me. I've never been so happy to hear the final bell. But the minute I reach my locker, I get a text.

I must groan out loud, because Saanvi and Holden lean in to read over my shoulder.

"I am NOT talking to her."

First I have the world's most humiliating video posted, and then I become a poster-child activist against bad internet memes? No thanks.

"You could . . ."

"Absolutely not." I can tell Saanvi's going to say that it might be useful. It might save other people from similar situations. But I just can't. "I can't handle one more single person knowing about this."

Holden shrugs. "No one reads that blog anyway."

Which isn't true. Everyone at The Mitch reads Miranda's blog. Holden proves this a minute later.

"Did either of you try that new ice cream place she recommended? I'm starving."

I sigh. "I can't eat ice cream. I have to go home and see if my mom has heard from the school."

"You want company?" Saanvi asks.

Holden looks horrified, probably at the thought of being in the room while my mom and I discuss my bra on the internet.

"Does your mom still buy those gourmet crackers?" Saanvi asks.

Which shows she's an absolute genius, because yes, my

mom does still buy those crackers, and Brie, and that's enough to convince Holden to join us.

Apparently, there's been no phone call. When Mom comes home, she has her post-yoga glow. She convinces Holden and Saanvi to stay for dinner, and seems completely happy stuffing us with fish tacos and guacamole, with Mexican chocolate torte for dessert.

The torte isn't exactly traditional. Mom made it in individual ramekins and decorated the tops with shiny pink candies.

"They're like disco tortes!" Saanvi says.

Mom laughs. "I should call them that on my menus."

She disappears into her room to catch up on work, after the three of us promise to handle the dishes.

"But not quite yet. I can't move," I tell Saanvi and Holden.

We're sprawled across the living room like overstuffed walruses, and our eating has disintegrated into picking the pink candies from the top of an extra torte and tossing them at one another.

"Hang on a sec," Holden says. He takes a photo of a leftover taco. Then he grabs my laptop and opens it on the coffee table, right in the middle of our mess.

"Don't spill stuff on my computer!" The school assigns our laptops, and I'm sure Ms. Plante wouldn't be happy to have Holden's torte crumbs sprinkled across my keyboard. "Another meeting with the principal is the last thing I need."

He ignores me.

"Are you listening?" I reach to nudge my computer farther away. Then I toss a pink candy at Holden. He catches it on his tongue like a frog.

"My turn!" Saanvi lines up on the couch behind him and I

aim a candy at her mouth. I miss and try again. The third time, Holden pops up and swallows it en route.

Saanvi can't stop laughing.

It gets worse when Holden grabs the laptop again and, after a minute, turns the screen toward me. He's transferred over the photo of my mom's taco, and it's now one of the Rocky Mountain peaks. It fits surprisingly well.

Saanvi snort-laughs.

"Okay, stop. The neighbors are going to complain."

But I'm laughing, too. It's almost enough to make me forget about the ache in my gut and the fact that everyone in the school has seen me strip, over and over again.

Almost, but not quite.

"Uh-oh," Holden says. He passes me his phone. The Mitch has sent a mass email.

Dear Mitchell Academy Families,

Please see the following information about ethical use of the internet at Mitchell Academy. Your child's online safety is our highest concern. As always, *securitas genera victoria*.

Prohibited:
• Use of the internet to transmit any materials in violation of board policies, local, provincial, or federal laws;
• Duplicating, storing, downloading, or sharing threatening, abusive, or obscene material.

Students are warned against the following:
• Sharing or revealing passwords;

- Using or attempting to use another person's user ID and/or password;
- Accessing or attempting to access any part of the system without authorization.

The electronic system is a shared resource and it must be used in a way that does not disrupt services to others. We encourage you to discuss this with your children.

Sincerely,

Mitchell Academy Administration

A minute later, my phone rings.

"Hi, George."

"The school sent an email, darling. Anything I need to worry about?"

"Nope." Absolutely nothing for my grandmother to worry about. Ever. "I'm here with Saanvi and Holden. They stayed for dinner."

"How lovely. Say hello for me, darling."

I hang up, feeling as if I've narrowly escaped. When I droop, Saanvi slings an arm around my shoulders.

"You're going to get through this. We'll do it together. Alright?"

I nod. I'm going to handle everything. But it feels like climbing a taco mountain. I wish I knew how, exactly, I'm supposed to do it.

———

It's after eight by the time we finish the dishes and Saanvi and Holden head home. Mom emerges from her room, pours herself a glass of wine, and flops onto the living room couch. I can tell in a glance that she hasn't had a call from Ms. Plante.

She never bothers to read the school emails.

She might not find out.

I drop onto the couch beside her. Once I'm there, I can see a stockpile of pink candies under our coffee table—the remains of our mini-food-fight. At this moment, picking them up seems like too much work.

Mom's phone buzzes and she glances at the text.

"Work?" I ask.

She shakes her head. "Frank's asking me out for a drink. Will you be alright?"

My insides could be served on one of her skewers, but I don't want to explain everything. If I do, I'll end up crying again, she'll cancel her date and call the school, and there will be another excruciating meeting with Ms. Plante. Then there's the issue of explaining to George how I wound up shirtless on video.

George is the one who actually pays for The Mitch. After this, she might decide on Swiss boarding school. Or Amish homeschool. Or Antarctica, which might not be so bad.

I force myself to nod. "Sure."

"You'll have to meet Frank soon, Dominica. He's quite luscious."

"Eww, Mom."

She laughs. "Alright, then. He's kind. And smart. And handsome."

Mom's brought home two or three guys over the years and they've all been . . . interesting.

I give her a long look. She's gorgeous. Her hair is naturally curly and falls in perfect tendrils. She has big dark eyes, long eyelashes, and perfect cheekbones.

"Do you ever get . . . unwanted attention?"

"Ugh," she says, shaking her head. "Men can be pigs sometimes."

"So what do you do about it?"

Mom's eyes narrow. "Does someone have a crush on you?"

I snort. The idea of me having that particular problem is sort of ridiculous. I might have the same genetic ingredients as Mom, but something went wrong in the execution. My soufflé flopped.

No, I have a different sort of issue.

"I'm filing information for future use," I tell her.

She nods and swings her feet around so she's sitting up straight. I can tell she's preparing to have a motherhood moment. I think she secretly likes these. Since I'm the one who keeps us organized around here, and she's the one most in need of a curfew, her chances are rare.

"The best thing to do is to avoid getting into a situation you can't control," she says. "That means sticking with your friends, making good decisions, and keeping your head clear." She pauses. "Is there drinking at your school? Or drugs? Frank says private schools are hotbeds for drugs."

"Mom! No one I know takes drugs."

I'm not sure any of Mom's advice would have saved me from having this video spread across the school. I wasn't drinking or taking drugs or in a bad situation. I was flipping my shirt right-side out! Maybe things have gotten more complicated since Mom was thirteen.

"I need to get ready." Mom stands and plants a kiss on my forehead. "You be careful out there, alright?"

She sounds like Lou.

"Always," I promise.

She's barely turned away when my phone buzzes.

> **MIRANDA:** Dom? I know this is a stressful time, but I think it would be helpful if people could hear your point of view.

Scowling at Miranda's text, I chuck my phone to the far side of the couch and pull my laptop toward me. I click on a YouTube video about making stencils, and watch as the instructor uses a knife to slice a design into sheets of thin, clear plastic called acetate. She uses a separate sheet for each color in her design.

It's nice to think about something unrelated to my life.

I'm so absorbed that I jump when Mom rushes back into the room. She's transformed herself into someone ten years younger. Short, cream-colored dress (Naples yellow light), wedge heels, dangly gold earrings. Any attention my mom draws tonight is entirely intentional.

"You be careful out there, too," I tell her.

She laughs as she heads out the door.

I put the laptop aside and drag myself off the couch to do a pink-candy cleanup. At least some messes are easy to fix.

When I'm done, I retrieve my phone from the couch cushions. There are texts waiting for me.

SAANVI: ♥ ♥ ♥

HOLDEN:

ME: Argh. Holden, you were right last year when you said the cameras were a terrible idea and an invasion of our privacy.

SAANVI: Wasn't he kind of a jerk? Didn't he say you'd been brainwashed?

HOLDEN: Sorry about that.

ME: And anxious. You also said I was anxious.

SAANVI: Which he's now going to feel guilty about basically forever.

HOLDEN: True.

ME: But you were right. Entirely, 100% right.

HOLDEN: You too.

ME: I don't think we can both be 100% right.

SAANVI: You can. Quantum physics.

ME: I'll take your word for it.

HOLDEN: Sorry.

ME: Me too.

ME: Also, Ms. Plante is a gorgon.

SAANVI: OMG. IKR??

I take my computer into my bedroom. This time, I don't search for more Banksy videos. Instead, I type a name into the Google search bar.

Graydon Cameron.

Immediately, a dozen photos appear. Graydon Cameron and my mom, holding giant drinks with pink paper umbrellas. Graydon Cameron in a leather jacket, standing beside a motorcycle. Graydon Cameron on the beach, holding a football. He isn't shy. In that image—the same one that sits on my mom's dresser—he's staring straight into the camera lens. His green eyes seem to sparkle with laughter.

Mom says I have his eyes.

She also says motorcycles are evil creations and if I ever get on one, she'll kill me. Which doesn't make logical sense, but I get what she means.

Graydon Cameron has never typed my name into a search bar, because he died in a motorcycle accident when I was a baby. One of the images that pops up on Google is the program from his funeral.

Every once in a while, I wonder what Graydon Cameron would think of me. He and Mom never even got married, but Mom says they were going to. She says once I was old enough, I would have been the flower girl at their wedding. Graydon Cameron probably would have taken me biking. Or taught me to ski. He might have loved even my lamest sketches.

It kind of sucks not having a dad.

Then again, the only thing worse than telling your mom about having your bra online would be telling your dad about having your bra online.

I click on the school forum.

The posts are still gone.

The posts are gone.

The posts are gone.

I toss the laptop aside and flop back on my bed. It's done. Maybe there will be a few more whispers and whistles, but everyone will forget soon.

I'll be an unknown entity again, with no social media accounts, no embarrassing posts, and no boobs on the internet.

They'll forget.

CHAPTER EIGHT
PROTEST ~~RIOT~~ RODENT

MOM'S IN THE KITCHEN on Friday morning. When I emerge from my room, she presents a plate of French toast with a proud flourish.

"I made your favorite!"

"I'm not really hungry." The thought of facing the school hallways again is making my stomach clench. I know my video was only posted two days ago, but I'd like everyone to hurry up and move on to other things.

"You've been so busy lately. They ask so much of you at that school! Have a few bites, at least."

Mom has an ulterior motive. I can tell by the way she's pasted on a super-wide smile.

Cautiously, I take a bite. It's delicious. It might even be worth whatever she's about to spring on me.

"So, I've invited Frank to dinner tomorrow."

Or not.

"Do you want me to go out with George?" Then Mom and Frank could have the apartment to themselves.

"No! I want you to meet him. You and George both. It's time."

Of course it is. Because the best way to end the worst week of my life is definitely to meet my mom's new boyfriend.

I shove a giant bite into my mouth to avoid having to

respond. This doesn't seem to faze Mom. She plants a kiss on my forehead and squeezes my shoulders.

"You're going to like him." Her super-wide smile gets even wider.

I think I manage to nod.

There are only a few random bursts of giggles when Saanvi, Holden, and I get to school, and people might be laughing about something else. I might be imagining the eyes on my back.

At least I have art first period. When I breathe in the smell of watercolor paints, I feel immediately calmer.

Until Ms. Crofton takes attendance.

"Marcus? Where is Marcus?" She scans the room as if he might be hiding.

"He hasn't been here for a couple days," someone says. "There was a video . . ."

Ms. Crofton immediately pales. For a moment, she stands frozen at the front of the class.

I notice she's not wearing one of her bamboo dresses today. Instead, she's in wide black dress pants and a long-sleeved sweater, with an art smock tied over top.

After a moment, she shakes her head. "Alright, I'll check in with Marcus later. Let's get out our sketchbooks and work on some initial ideas."

I have a half hour of perfect, blissful quiet before we're interrupted by Ms. Marcie on the public address system.

"Attention all students. Please pardon the interruption. There will be an assembly in the auditorium, starting in ten minutes. I repeat, an assembly in the auditorium, beginning in ten minutes."

I find Holden and Saanvi in the middle of the crowded hallway. I glance around as I join them; no one seems to be staring at me.

"They've moved on to new dramas," Holden whispers, reading my mind.

"Fingers crossed."

"Why the sudden assembly?" Saanvi asks.

"As long as we're not publicly discussing my forum post, I don't care." We couldn't be, right?

As we file into a long row of flip-down theater seats, I feel a bit safer. In the front row, there's a line of VIP visitors, their gray hair perfectly parted. A few bald heads reflect the light. I'm pretty sure they're too old to know about the internet.

Ms. Plante takes the stage, taps her microphone, and begins her usual spiel about *securitas genera victoria*.

"Security breeds success." She turns her smile like a spotlight to the front row. "That motto guides all our decisions here at Mitchell Academy."

As she begins listing statistics about the eradication of vandalism and bullying, Saanvi leans toward me.

"You were right about Josh," she whispers. "His username and the anonymous one who posted your video are linked. Definitely the same person."

Ugh. I don't even want to think about this.

"From top to bottom, inside and out, Mitchell Academy is designed for the enriched pursuit of academic excellence," Ms. Plante says.

"So he posted it?" I whisper.

Saanvi nods. She looks angrier than ever.

Holden leans across. "You got something? Who?"

"Josh."

My stomach drops. I was the one who suggested that Josh might be involved, but now the full implications sink in. Josh treats the school like his own personal kingdom. He has enough access—to his mom's office, for example—to accomplish something like this. And he's basically untouchable.

"I can't stand that guy," Holden says.

At the front, Ms. Plante welcomes one of the guests onto the stage.

"This is Mr. Sousa from Infinity Security. He'll be working with Mitchell Academy this month to help create and maintain safe online spaces for all of our students."

Crap. We *are* discussing the forum posts.

"Whoa. That was fast," Holden mutters.

"It can't possibly be related," Saanvi says.

"This is all because of me!"

Someone shushes us.

At the front, Mr. Sousa is talking about internet safety and not posting naked pictures of yourself online. Of course he is.

My face burns, and I'm thankful it's too dark in here for Holden to classify the color.

"This isn't all about you," Saanvi hisses. "She can't have hired an internet company and arranged a presentation that quickly."

Mr. Sousa extends both arms, as if he's going to hug the entire student body. "We are all looking forward to working with you."

I've never been so happy to have an assembly end. Except

that as we file from the auditorium, Saanvi and Holden go back to talking about Josh.

"Not a huge surprise," Holden says.

Saanvi nods. "His was the first account I checked, but it took a few days to get past the log-in page and confirm it."

Of course it was Josh. Last year, there was a computer glitch and the entire school got straight As in math. The letters that went home explaining the "software error" never fully dampened the rumors that Josh had somehow accessed the system.

Which makes me wonder. "Did you actually hack the school computers to figure out who hacked the school computers?"

Saanvi shushes me.

"I knew you were good at programming, but this is impressive," I tell her.

"It's not that hard. Which is the scary part. I shouldn't be able to get in, and neither should Josh."

"Can we rob banks now? Or jewelry stores?" Holden asks.

"Dom would faint the first time we tried." Saanvi rolls her eyes.

"Very funny." Though probably true.

"Can we get back to Josh?" Saanvi says.

"Can we get back *at* Josh?" Holden suggests.

"I guess seeing Principal Plante again would be a waste," I say.

"Total," Holden says. "We need to go directly to the source."

Then, as if Josh is Voldemort and speaking his name has made him appear, we round the corner and find him and his posse clustered in the hall outside the math room.

Saanvi doesn't hesitate. She steps directly in front of him. "We need to talk."

His entire group falls silent.

I consider dropping to the floor and trying to crawl away. It wouldn't work, though. And my crawling would probably be caught on video, go viral, and make my life even worse.

Josh shrugs at Saanvi. "If you need me that badly, all you have to do is ask."

He waggles his eyebrows at his friends in a way that makes them laugh.

Holden looks as if he's stepped in dog poop.

Saanvi seems like she might explode.

"Maybe we should go talk to your mom. Together," she says, her words low and menacing.

"Talking to the principal is an excellent option, if you're going to skip second period."

It's Mr. Nowak, and his gravel voice makes us all jump. Where did he come from? He stands in the center of the hallway, arms crossed over his chest.

"To class. Now!"

Saanvi and I immediately scoot down the hallway. Holden saunters in the other direction, toward art.

"Chop, chop, Mr. LaClaire."

"I swear that man is stalking us!" Saanvi says before she splits off, heading for the computer lab.

I barely breathe all the way to gym. If I could get enough air into my lungs, I might scream. I'm not so embarrassed anymore, I realize. Now I'm furious. There's pent-up adrenaline zooming around inside me.

My phone buzzes.

I still hate the thought of talking to Miranda. But I have to do *something* or I'm going to self-combust. My hands are shaking.

I slow as I reach the hallway outside the gym. A dozen basketballs pound from the floor and the walls, and shouts echo as someone shoots.

I can't go in there. Not in this state.

There's a camera mounted to the left of the double doors, pointed along the hall. If I stand directly beneath it, I should be invisible.

I glance around. No other cameras.

When Banksy's angry, he channels it into art.

My heart beats loudly in my ears as I dig for a marker in my backpack. If I don't find one, I'm not supposed to do this. If I do find one . . .

This doesn't even make sense.

My hand closes around a marker.

I glance quickly up and down the hall once more. There's no one in sight.

I still have a video-game-style map of the school cameras in my mind. Once I started noticing them, I couldn't stop. Each camera can "see" in a cone shape, narrow near the camera lens and wider farther away. Depending on how close the cameras are to one another, some of the cones overlap. Some of them have gaps in between.

This exact spot is a gap. There's a camera above me, but its cone radiates along the hallway, not directly down the wall.

As I stand in the blind spot, marker clenched in my fist, I remember a word. *Panopticon.* It's a word I think Banksy might like. Holden's mom would approve, definitely. She was the one who taught it to me.

Last year, when the cameras were first going in, Holden's mom was dead-set against them. I remember talking to her about it in her kitchen. Her fancy, ultra-modern but still Victorian kitchen.

Ms. LaClaire has what George calls "presence." She takes up space. That afternoon, she was wearing a long, flowered caftan that on anyone else would have looked ridiculous, but that somehow made her seem even more creative and brilliant than usual.

"I ordered this spectacular new coffee machine," she told Holden and me. "What would you like? Americanos? Espressos? Lattes?"

Holden chose an espresso, so I did the same, even though I wasn't sure what that would turn out to be. I don't even like coffee.

His mom hit buttons. The machine ground and whirred.

"And how was lunch at the Sunshine Spot?" she asked, arranging three tiny white mugs on the counter.

"How did you know we were at the spot?" Holden asked. It was one of those rare sunny Saturdays in February and we'd met Saanvi for a walk on the beach and then stopped for lunch at a diner on 4th Avenue. One of those diners that looks old-fashioned but costs a fortune.

"The panopticon, darling," Holden's mom said.

I assumed this was another coffee variety, but apparently not.

"Seriously," he said.

"Eyes everywhere." When she raised her brows, she looked exactly like her son.

"The what-i-con?" I asked.

"Don't get her started," Holden said.

"The panopticon was a prison designed by Jeremy Bentham. Brilliant thinking, though in this case his ideas took a rather sinister turn. The prison was designed like a wheel. The prisoners would live along the edges and the guards in the center. From the core, they could see what any prisoner was doing, at any time."

"See? Creepy," Holden told me. He took a small sip of his espresso. I did the same and almost choked. It was insanely bitter.

"The prisoners never knew when they were being watched, so they had to assume they were under surveillance at all times," Ms. LaClaire said.

"Story of my life," Holden said.

She laughed. "Well, the panopticon was never built. And in this case, your dad happened to drive by the café as you were going inside."

Which was a relief of sorts. I didn't like the idea that Holden's mother had us under secret surveillance. But I didn't think much more about the panopticon, back then.

The panopticon seems perfectly relevant now.

Inside the gym, the noise has dampened a little. It sounds like there's only one basketball now, and an actual game going on. I can hear the shouts for the ball, and the hammer of shoes on the polished floor.

Around me, the hallway's still empty.

I turn toward the wall and the camera and reach as high as I can underneath the lens. I start with the outline of a rat, like Banksy, but that seems like copying. Then I remember the squirrel I drew in the bathroom cubicle.

It takes only a minute to turn my rat into a squirrel. The squeak of the marker against the white paint of the wall seems extra-loud, but I keep going.

THE PANOPTICON, I write beneath.

One more time, I scan up and down the hallway. Completely clear. I stuff the marker back into my bag. My hands are shaking again, twice as badly. But I feel strangely better than I did a few minutes ago. Like something that was tied too tightly inside me has released a little.

I head down the hall to the girls' changeroom, swing open the doors and . . .

Oomph.

I run smack into Ana. We rebound in opposite directions, her binder flying open onto the hallway floor.

"What are you—"

"Sorry!"

I recover first and reach for her binder, but she scrambles toward me on her hands and knees and tries to snatch it away. The corner of it catches on my bracelet.

"Wait," I say.

"Let go—"

It's hard to extricate myself when she's pulling on the binder at the same time. Then the strings of my bracelet break, and tiny blue beads go flying, half into the hallway and half onto the grimy tiles of the changeroom.

"Oh no! Sorry!" She sounds sincere.

"It's okay. It was a garage-sale find."

I turn back to the binder. Without meaning to, I see the pages that have spilled from the cover. The top one says, in pink block letters, underlined twice: PASSWORD. Written underneath in turquoise ink is a string of numbers. A Fibonacci sequence. Probably no one but me would recognize it.

Ana scoops everything up and leaps to her feet, clutching the binder to her chest.

I can't do anything except stare at her.

"I'm late," she says, and scurries down the hall.

What was she doing in the changeroom, I wonder? And why is she wandering around with codes in her binder?

It's enough to keep my mind churning for the rest of the day. That, and ideas for more drawings. And thoughts about the panopticon.

I'm not the only one who's busy. Before the bell rings, an alert pops up on my screen. There's a new blog post available.

The Mitch Mash
Hackers Strike Havoc
by Miranda Bowen

Several people were targeted earlier this week on the Mitchell Academy's forums. Anonymous users uploaded inappropriate videos of four students and one teacher.

"It's really hurtful," said one of the students targeted. He's asked that his name not be published in order to protect his privacy.

"What's left of it," he said.

"You'd like to think people are good, and then something like this happens," said another student.

"This is a horrific, complete violation of students' privacy rights," said Saanvi Agarwal, a close friend of one victim. "I think the school should take immediate action, and whoever did this should be expelled."

Art teacher Ms. Crofton was unaware of the forum posts until recently, but has promised swift action. "When I find who put up those videos, we'll be having a long chat about values," she said.

Ms. Plante declined to comment.

CHAPTER NINE
MOB MENTALITY

I THROW MYSELF into a chair at our cafeteria table. Saanvi sets her tray beside mine, looking as if she might murder someone. Holden—wisely—says nothing. He takes a bite of his Friday Surprise cafeteria special, looks back and forth between us, then waits.

"I can tell Josh posted the video, just by the smirk on his face," I say.

"I thought we were going to let things slide and hope everyone forgets about this," Holden says.

Saanvi mutters some questionable vocabulary words.

"What if they don't move on? What if they're planning something worse? Did you hear them talking in humanities?"

I tell them about Josh bragging that he was going to rack up a billion points.

"They're probably running a football pool," Holden says.

"It's April."

"Betting on baseball, then."

"Holden! It's not baseball!" Saanvi says.

He sighs. "What are we supposed to do about it?"

Fortunately, I've already figured this out. I figured it out while holding my breath between the gym and here. "You need to go undercover," I tell him.

Saanvi snaps her fingers and points at me. "Excellent idea."

"Terrible idea!" Holden says. He looks like we've asked him to roll in a pigsty.

But he could find out what's going on. Easily.

Although it's supposed to be all about academics, our school is actually all about money. "Mitchell Academy is designed for the enriched pursuit of academic excellence," Ms. Plante said at the assembly. It would have been more accurate if she'd replaced "enriched" with "filthy rich." And while Saanvi comes from a well-off family, and George never seems to blink at my tuition bill, Holden is loaded. Fully, obscenely, ridiculously rich.

To people like Josh, that means everything.

Holden still looks appalled.

"We need to know what's going on," I say.

"This will end sooner if we leave them alone," he insists.

"Really? Are we going to wait for another video?" Saanvi asks.

He can't hold out for long against both of us.

Although he tries. "I'm not like those guys. I'm not one of them."

"Of course you're not," I say. "But you can pretend."

I don't understand why he's making a big deal of this. We're not asking him to get a bathroom wedgie or have his butt shoved in a locker. Holden is every bit as cool as Josh or Max. Twice as artistic and probably twice as coordinated, too.

"Unless you're scared." Saanvi's eyebrows arc in an evil way, which I resolve to practice in the mirror when I get home.

Holden grunts.

"If you get drawn into a life of crime, and a mobster wraps

you in bricks and tosses you in the ocean, I will personally swim down and fish your body from the depths," I tell him.

"And I'll rush to your side with emergency blankets," Saanvi adds.

When he sighs, I know we've won.

"Give me a day or two. I'll see what I can find out. NO promises."

It doesn't exactly have me brimming with confidence, but at least it's something.

We're about to leave the table when our phones simultaneously buzz. Saanvi's the first to grab hers.

"It's Ana."

"She's texting us from across the room?" I can see Ana, two tables over. When she notices me looking, she waves manically.

ANA: Hey guys! Got your numbers from Miranda. We're planning a meet-up at Cheesecake Castle tomorrow night! Can you come?

HOLDEN: Already booked, sry. Have fun.

ME: Meeting my mom's new boyfriend. 😨

ANA: Wow! Hope he's great! 😊

SAANVI: Miranda's coming tomorrow?

ANA: Yup! Me, Miranda, and tiramisu cheesecake!

SAANVI: k, I'll try.

ANA: YAY!!!

Ana waves again, with both hands this time.

I glance at Saanvi. "Are you really going tomorrow?"

She blushes, which makes very little sense.

"With Ana?" I try not to sound incredulous, but I'm pretty sure I fail.

"And Miranda. It's a good chance to talk, outside of school. You know, about her blog posts and stuff."

Which would sort of make sense, if Saanvi weren't still a vivid Toluidine red.

I'm about to ask more when there's a burst of laughter from Josh's table. One of the guys is shimmying out of his shirt in slow motion.

It's entirely stupid, but that doesn't stop me from turning the same shade as Saanvi.

"C'mon. Let's get out of here," Holden says.

He grabs my hand as the three of us weave our way from the cafeteria. Part of me wants to collapse on his shoulder and cry, but that would be letting Josh win.

I suck in a deep breath and disengage my hand.

"I should get ready for class." I need a few minutes of quiet, just me and my mental map of the school's blind spots.

"Those guys are jerks!" Saanvi calls after me.

I'm too busy fast-blinking to look back at her.

———

I draw another squirrel while on a "bathroom break" in the middle of third period. I put him in an alcove just around the corner from the office. The whole time, I'm sure Ms. Plante's heels will clack-clack around the corner and she'll catch me, but she doesn't. I draw this new squirrel as if it's been caught in a searchlight. *THE PANOPTICON*, I write beneath him.

I'm getting strangely attached to these squirrels.

Saanvi's mom idles in front of the school in her black Mercedes.

"Hello, my artistes!" she calls, waving to the two of us so enthusiastically that Saanvi cringes. Saanvi's Labrador retriever, Lucky, has his huge head out the passenger-side window. He looks equally excited to see us.

"My brain is tired," I say once we've climbed into the back seat. (Lucky refuses to relinquish the front.)

I let my head fall onto Saanvi's shoulder. She puts a hand on my head, I put my hand on top of hers, and we sit in the back seat like a shoulder, head, hand, and hand sandwich until her mom swings into the parking lot of the arts center.

"What are you working on, girls?" Mrs. Agarwal asks. "Perspective again, or something new?"

"Shading," Saanvi tells her.

"Oooh," she says, as if shading is art's most exciting innovation. "How interesting!"

Saanvi's mom is a well-known arts patron, which basically means she gives scads of money to the ballet, the city art museum, and the theater. When she and George found each other at The Mitch orientation, they were almost as happy as

Saanvi and I were. And before you could say Picasso, we were sharing private lessons at Beaux Arts. It's entirely across the city from The Mitch, but Mrs. Agarwal never seems to mind.

"Thanks for the ride," I tell her.

"Go and be great!" she says.

We hold onto our smiles as we close the SUV door, but we give matching sighs as we head for class.

"I have the artistic talent of a chicken," Saanvi says.

This is true. And while I usually love our lessons together, today I feel as if all the energy's been leached from my body.

"Okay, let's think of this as our outlet," Saanvi says. "We'll get all our feels out."

Unfortunately, our instructor makes that difficult. Andrei doesn't see art as an outlet. To him, it's a calling.

"Now you varm up, girls," he calls in his thick Romanian accent. "Qvick, qvick. Vithout lifting your hand from ze paper."

This is our usual warm-up exercise. It might be sort of fun, if Andrei didn't critique as he walked by.

"Commitment," he shouts as he passes behind Saanvi.

"Less theenking, girls. Trust, only trust."

As soon as I think about not thinking, I'm bombarded with thoughts. My fingers get confused.

"You know, it's not just your videos that have disappeared. The entire forum's shut down, homework discussions and all." Saanvi starts whispering the minute Andrei busies himself with organizing pencils. "Ms. Plante must have done it."

This is good news, at least. I don't want to log on to the forums ever again.

"Dominica, maybe you break vist as child?"

When I stare blankly up at Andrei, he mimes a gnarled hand. "Not just vist. Use your arm, shoulder!"

I sigh and adjust my posture until he nods grudgingly.

"Did your parents hear anything?" I whisper when he wanders away again. "My mom never got a call."

"Nothing."

Andrei shakes his head at Saanvi. "Vhat, are you ballerina? Zis is supposed to be graceful? You are not touching zee paper. Commit!"

I snort, then Saanvi snorts, then neither of us can hold our pencils upright.

"Focus," Andrei demands.

I do *try* to focus for the next few minutes, and I at least avoid being called a ballerina. After a while, Andrei either decides we've learned something, or that we're hopeless. Probably the latter. He sets us free to work on our own sketches.

I wait until he's absorbed at his easel.

"So what do we do about Josh?" I whisper.

"Hang him by his fingernails."

"I love when you get feisty."

"Feisty is a sexist word."

"Is it?"

"Do you ever call guys 'feisty'? Would you say that about Holden?" she asks.

"Well, Holden is entirely un-feisty. But I get your point."

"I'm angry."

Without her usual adjectives, it sounds even sharper.

"Me too." I realize it's true at the same time as I say it. "We *should* be angry."

"I'm going to find out how Josh got these videos," she says.

97

"Okay. And then? Revenge?"

"I haven't figured that out yet. I'll let you know."

"Here's to anger," I say.

We click our pencils together as if already toasting to her success.

Then I look back at my picture, and I realize I've drawn a panopticon squirrel. Quickly, I tear the page from my drawing pad before Saanvi can see it.

Andrei glances over. Saanvi raises her eyebrows at me.

"Starting over!" I chirp.

But when I lift my pencil to the paper, my fingers are shaking.

I'm angry. There's a compressed ball of rage sitting in my chest and if I let it escape, I'm not sure what will happen.

Now's not the time, I know that much.

I force myself to draw something happy. A long-eared bunny stealing vegetables.

Andrei is not impressed. "Ziz is not your best vork," he says, next time he walks behind us.

Zis is entirely true.

Mom's still sound asleep when I wake up on Saturday morning. I pour myself a bowl of cereal and sit at the table, clicking through my texts. There's a new notification from Miranda's blog.

The Mitch Mash
Forum Fiasco
by Miranda Bowen

Administrators have closed the student forums indefinitely, after several security breaches last week. Five inappropriate videos were anonymously posted.

"The forums are to be used responsibly, for organizing student activities and coordinating group projects. This sort of misuse will not be tolerated," Principal Plante wrote to this reporter, via email on Friday evening.

Asked when the forums might reopen, she said the matter would be discussed with the PAC and the school's board of directors.

Meanwhile, some students are concerned that their studies will suffer. "This poses a serious disadvantage to those of us who prefer to work collaboratively," said eighth-grader Ana Kavanaugh.

Fellow eighth-grader Josh Plante echoed her opinions: "Sucks, dude."

Don't expect the forums to reopen anytime soon. The next meeting of the Mitchell Academy parents' association is more than two weeks away, on Monday, May 13.

I roll my eyes at the quotes from Josh and Ana. Typical. Then I set my phone aside and vow not to think about the stupid forums for the rest of the day. My brain needs a break, and George has invited me shopping for the morning. I don't normally love shopping, but today it might be the perfect distraction.

A couple hours later, when Mom is still in her housecoat, sipping coffee, George buzzes from downstairs. We set off for our retail therapy session.

When she parks in front of the posh stores along Robson Street, it feels as if we've escaped into another world. I try to forget school and Josh and the video—everything. Here, the only things that matter are whether a teal sweater will go with the beige pants George has at home in her closet, and whether owning two of the same tank top is practical (me) or unimaginative (George).

We end up extending our date so we can have lunch and see a matinee. When we finally get back to the apartment, carrying a half-dozen store loyalty cards, a new cardigan (leopard-print rather than teal), and a tank top in an unusual peach color (our eventual compromise), there's classical music playing. The air smells faintly of cologne.

This weekend, Mom's everybody-meet-Frank Saturday dinner has replaced our usual La Patisserie Sunday brunch.

"Mom?"

"We're in here!" she calls. "Come and say hello!"

I hang George's sweater for her, then I pick up Mom's sunglasses from the floor. George hovers behind me. Maybe we're both procrastinating.

"There you are!" Mom smiles when we finally get to the living room. She and Frank nestle side by side on the couch, goblets of wine on the coffee table in front of them.

Frank stands to shake our hands. He's tall and thin, with a slightly receding hairline.

"Georgina, a pleasure to meet you," he says, kissing her cheek. "And Dominica, your mother raves about you."

"Not in the lunatic way, I hope."

He looks confused.

"As in 'raving lunatic'?" I explain.

"Uh . . . no. I believe she thinks quite highly of you."

Kill me now. I already know what I'm going to tell Holden: Frank has the sense of humor of a tree stump.

George perches on the edge of the recliner, crossing her ankles as if she's the queen of England. Frank settles himself back onto the couch and puts an arm around Mom's shoulders. And I'm not sure what to do with myself, because I am certainly not sitting on the couch with the two of them.

"I'll put dinner in the oven while you three get acquainted," Mom says.

She's practically glowing. We all watch her float from the room.

This leaves me space on the couch. Beside Frank. There's really no way to avoid it.

"How did you two meet?" I ask, squeezing myself as far toward the armrest as possible.

"At an event," he says. "I was enjoying an appetizer—a delicious appetizer—when your mother appeared on the other side of the table."

"It was the yoga studio's open house!" Mom calls from the kitchen. "Remember in March, when I donated the nibbles?"

"What kind of law do you practice?" George asks.

"Wasn't that just fate?" Mom interrupts, returning with one of her specialties—Lebanese carrot dip and pita triangles.

"Must have been," I agree. Though I'm quite sure people don't end up at yoga-studio open houses because of fate. Fate is not that cruel.

"And your area of law?" George asks again.

"Civil rights," he says.

George looks impressed, and Mom smacks a kiss on Frank's cheek.

I try not to roll my eyes.

"Tell me more about yourself, Dominica." His voice goes perfectly with his navy suit and his red tie: polished, smooth, and possibly a bit slippery. I'm withholding judgment.

"Interests? Clubs? Sports teams?"

"I take art lessons. Did you say civil rights?" I ask.

"He helps keep people safe," Mom says. "Refugees, or environmental activists. He's even been on the news."

"It's not that glamorous," he says. "Mostly it's paperwork."

I wonder if there's a law that says your bra can't be posted on a school forum. If Holden can prove that Josh posted my video, maybe I can have him thrown in prison. Solitary confinement. A life of gruel and water.

Except then I'll have to go to court and explain how I decided to flip my shirt right-side-out in the middle of a library, thus flashing the security cameras. So maybe not.

". . . basically means that everyone should be treated equally," Frank says, "regardless of skin color, gender, sexual orientation. That sort of thing. We also do free speech cases."

"Privacy?"

"That too," he says.

There's a brief pause while I consider all of this. Frank reaches for the hardcover book upside down on the coffee table . . . my Banksy book, I realize. I must have left it there.

I have to resist the urge to snatch it from his hands. I'm

kind of in love with it. I've already told George not to give me a new title this week, because I'm not relinquishing this one.

"An interesting fellow," Frank says, scanning the pages. Then he smiles. "Someone who might be in need of a civil rights lawyer one day."

"Do you know his work, Frank?" George asks, leaning forward.

"Doesn't everyone? Did you hear about the stand in New York, where he gave away those signed prints for ten dollars, and no one realized they were getting original Banksys?"

George nods eagerly. I can see her being won over, sentence by sentence. Soon, they're talking about a violin virtuoso who played in a Washington, DC, subway, without anyone recognizing him.

"Only a few children stopped," George says.

I'm done listening, because I'm still thinking about Banksy.

"Excuse me for a minute," I tell George and Frank, not that they hear me. Sweeping up my book on the way past, I head for my room.

"Don't disappear!" Mom calls as I pass the kitchen. "Dinner's almost ready!"

"Back in a sec," I tell her.

I close my door and lean against it. The tight ball is roiling in my chest again. Angry, not feisty, Saanvi said. I'm angry.

I drop the Banksy book on my bed and flip through the pages until I find the piece I've been thinking about.

It's an angel painted in honor of Ozone, another graffiti artist. After Banksy painted the image, he posted a note on his website about it. He said that he'd originally painted "a crap picture" of two gunmen in banana costumes. Then his friend Ozone wrecked it, and left a note scrawled in the corner.

"If it's better next time I'll leave it."

Ozone was killed by an underground train, maybe while planning his next piece.

Banksy must take criticism well. He put his tribute angel to Ozone in the exact same spot. He said the world had lost a fearless graffiti writer and a "pretty perceptive art critic."

The note makes me think that Banksy must be a good sort of friend. Can you have friends when you're anonymous?

But if he does have friends, they probably know all about him, and he trusts them to keep his secrets. They protect one another.

I think about Holden, who agreed to hang out with Josh and Max.

I think about Saanvi, willing to confront Josh in the middle of the school hallway, even when he was surrounded by his goons.

I'd create tribute artworks for them. I might even throw myself in front of a train.

I flip through a few more Banksy projects. Even in this world of cameras everywhere, and social media tracking, and ID tags and border checks, he jets around anonymously, unnoticed until his artwork catches someone's eye. Banksy would hate the "Shotz" channel in the forums. He would hate the striptease video.

I grow more and more certain that Banksy wouldn't let his friends fight battles for him. He wouldn't sit around doing nothing after people were harassed on a chat forum. And he wouldn't quietly wait for things to get better.

"Dom! Dinner's ready!"

"Be right there!"

I hear Frank's voice from the dining table. "This looks amazing, Carol."

Before I lose my courage, I jot a to-do list. I'll have to get supplies, talk to Holden and Saanvi, walk through the school and check my mental map of the cameras one more time . . .

Thank goodness I forgot to hand in my project proposal to Ms. Sutton yesterday. I flip through my binder, but I can't find it. It doesn't matter. I'll write something else.

"Dom?"

"Coming!"

I'm going to have to change things entirely.

CHAPTER TEN
ON THE RECORD

SAANVI AND I meet up after dinner on Sunday to finish our math homework, but I get distracted delving into Saanvi's cheesecake outing with Ana and Miranda. She's being really weird about it.

"It was fine," she says. And then she looks away at the corner of the room. If this were a TV crime show, she'd definitely be hiding something.

"Fine? Just fine?"

"We were studying."

"With Ana."

"She's not so bad."

I stare at her. She spent hours with two of the world's most annoying prodigies.

"It was surprisingly fun."

"Okay, what really happened?"

"It was just cheesecake! I had salted caramel. I don't know what else you want me to tell you."

I stare at her for a little longer, but she opens her math workbook and starts working so diligently that I eventually give up. For now.

We've gotten through most of the assignment when we get a text from Holden, begging us to visit.

SAANVI: Come to Dom's place instead. We have chips.

HOLDEN: Can't. Move.

ME: It's late!

HOLDEN: SOS

SAANVI: Your mom won't be happy.

HOLDEN: Mayday.

HOLDEN: Too weak to type more . . .

I yell to my mom that Holden's having a homework emergency.

"Can we just run over there for twenty minutes?"

"It's already dark," she says, sticking her head around the corner from the kitchen.

"I'll take my phone and we'll stay together."

She purses her lips. "Twenty minutes."

Saanvi and I scramble for our shoes before she can change her mind.

SAANVI: On our way!

HOLDEN: Let yourselves in. I'm too tired to get to the door.

Saanvi rolls her eyes. "He's joking, right?"

He must be. "He's being ridiculous."

It's almost nine and his house looks dark. I feel like we're burglars as Saanvi types in the key code and we let ourselves through the French doors at the back. I can hear voices from the living room.

"Is that the TV?" Saanvi whispers.

"A film," I say in a snooty voice. "Holden's parents wouldn't watch TV."

Suddenly a blue light glows, and a woman's British accent fills the room. "Looking for films? I can suggest the following—"

"Shhhh!" Saanvi tries to shush the LaClaires' virtual assistant, but it's too late. The little white cylinder has already whirred into action.

"—this week's releases, what's new on Netflix, foreign films. Based on your previous choices, you might like—"

The kitchen light flicks on as Mr. and Mrs. LaClaire arrive in the doorway.

"Ah, it's you two. I should have known!" Holden's dad grins at us.

"Cancel," Mrs. LaClaire tells the virtual assistant.

"Sorry to disturb you," I say.

"A little late for a visit, isn't it?"

Fortunately, I have my math worksheets in my bag.

"We're dropping off homework," I say, tugging them out.

Once they wave us upstairs, we giggle our way to Holden's room.

"I almost jumped out of my skin when that thing turned on," I say.

"I know!"

Then we open Holden's bedroom door and step into another dimension.

Two years ago, Holden painted his entire room black, heritage wainscoting and all. His parents let him do this because he was "expressing his creativity," which apparently trumped their authentic antique decor. Once the room was black, Holden taped glow-in-the-dark stars everywhere. Lately, though, most of his stars have come unstuck.

At one stage, he was going to stencil his favorite poetry onto the walls. I was hanging out in his room when he started, choosing a poem that was completely inappropriate for sixth-graders.

His mom came in as he was finishing a line with the F-word in it.

"Oh, I just adore Lorna's work," she said.

Holden looked like she'd punctured his rebellion balloon, and that was the end of his poetry idea.

Tonight, he looks as if he's been punctured again. Plus, he stinks.

"Are you alright?" Saanvi sits on his desk chair and swivels back and forth, apparently taking in the disaster area that serves as his carpet. There are piles of dirty laundry in the corners, books strewn on the floor with their spines cracked open, and a teetering pile of dirty dishes near the door.

Holden is sprawled on his back across his bed. "I sacrificed my body for you."

"That sounds . . . uncomfortable."

"Pick-up basketball with Josh and Max," he says. "It *was* uncomfortable. You have no idea."

It would be highly unsanitary to sit on Holden's floor, so I perch at the edge of his bed.

"It's all about points," he says.

"Basketball?"

He props himself on his elbows and looks at me. "No, not basketball. I went undercover like you said."

"And?"

"It's a contest. Everyone's going to get points for the most embarrassing moments caught on film. A shot of someone scratching their butt might be worth one point. A shot of teachers making out in the staff room would be five points."

"Teachers were making out in the staff room? Who?" Saanvi asks.

He waves a hand in the air, then lets it flop back onto the mattress as if it's too heavy to hold up. "Just an example."

"So my video was part of some stupid contest?"

"Not according to them. No one's claiming credit for your video. Max didn't seem to know who accessed it. You *inspired* their contest."

"Wow. I'm so glad I can be motivational." Except entirely not. I squeeze my eyes shut for a moment.

"But the post came from Josh's account," Saanvi insists.

"If it was him, he wasn't bragging about it."

Even though Principal Plante deleted the forum post, my video's still making the rounds via text. Just this afternoon, three people sent it to me with notes like "thought you should know." As if I might not realize my bra is having a cyber crisis. As if I don't feel nauseated every time I think about it.

"It's not on Facebook, right?" I look at Saanvi miserably.

"It's not anywhere public. I've been checking."

"Unless it counts as public to have Josh flashing his phone screen around," Holden says.

I groan. "This is all a game to them."

"Bingo."

Which seems too happy a word.

"How can you be so calm about this?" Saanvi scowls at Holden. "It makes me want to riot. Or at least sue someone."

"I'm not calm," Holden says, completely calmly. "I just don't see how this helps Dom, or what we can do about it. Principal Plante will cover for Josh, if he started this."

He's right. Josh's mom is *not* objective. If the Pacific Ocean represented objectivity, she'd be way over on the Atlantic. Last winter, after Josh didn't get chosen for the school's wrestling team, Principal Plante cancelled the team's travel funding.

None of this makes things better. But I have my plan, now.

"You know, Josh is *one* of the problems . . ."

"A massive, obnoxious problem," Saanvi interrupts.

"And if someone else gave him my video, or posted it with his account, that person is a problem, too."

"I still think it was him," she says.

"But listen," I say. "These people aren't the only problems. It's the cameras. If the school wasn't watching us all the time, there wouldn't be videos to post."

"YOU'RE SO ENTIRELY RIGHT!" Saanvi jumps from her chair and starts pacing Holden's room. "Let's start a petition to get the cameras removed. Or talk to Miranda about a media blitz."

A media blitz. Just what we need. My video will be everywhere. Maybe they'll put one of those fuzzy boxes over my face, but everyone will know it's me. Me and my bra on TV.

"I think we need something more subtle . . . ," I manage.

She doesn't seem to hear me. "Or hold a march. A massive one. And I still want to get Josh expelled, even if you say he's not the main problem."

If she would slow down for a minute, I'd tell them about the squirrels. I should have told them last week. I don't know why I didn't, except that the artwork seemed a little silly. I guess I was drawing them to make myself feel a bit better, not to solve the camera issue. Or the Josh issue, for that matter. But now, things are going to change.

Saanvi's phone buzzes.

"Argh. My mom's looking for me."

She types a few words. "She's meeting me outside. I have to go."

"But I need to talk about—"

She doesn't seem to hear. "Thanks for the info, Holden. Even if it sucks."

Saanvi shuts the door behind her.

I feel myself deflate. I wanted to tell her what I'm planning, but now she's gone and Holden's basically comatose.

"I guess I'd better go, too."

"Don't even think about leaving!" he says, eyes snapping open. "How can you abandon me in this state? Especially now that Saanvi's gotten me all riled up."

"You don't look riled up. You look like you're going to pass out."

"It was a long day. And my legs hurt. And my arms. Also my right elbow. And—"

Holden has his own ensuite, which is slightly less disgusting than the rest of his room because a housekeeper cleans the bathrooms once a week. I find an empty crystal glass, refill it, and set it on his end table beside his phone.

"Thank you for your sacrifice," I tell him.

He grabs my hand as I turn to go.

"Hey," he says.

"Um . . . hey."

"I'm just . . . I'm sorry this video stuff happened. It wasn't fair," he says.

I've held it together pretty well all week. I put on a brave face for my mom and George. After the one small puking incident, I managed to ignore the whispers at school. I didn't cry in Principal Plante's office. Much.

But at this moment, when Holden apologizes for something that's entirely not his fault, and he says it like he'd make it all go away if he could, I almost lose it.

Then a text comes through on his phone. I don't mean to look. But because I'm still standing beside his end table . . .

It's a text from Miranda.

MIRANDA: You awake, handsome?

I disentangle my fingers from his and hand him the phone. He looks at the screen for a second too long.

"I have to go. I'll see you tomorrow morning," I say.

He tosses the phone onto his blankets. "What? Why? We could watch a movie. Can't you call your mom and tell her you'll be late?"

I slide away and make a break for the door. I'm gritting my

teeth so hard that there's no chance of crying. Or very little chance. Or, okay, maybe a minor chance, but not until I'm out the door and down the stairs and into the street. I know I told my mom that Saanvi and I would be together the whole time, but at this moment I'm entirely grateful to be alone in the dark where no one can see me.

By the time I get to the end of Holden's block, I'm done with sniveling. I'm back to planning street art. Or school art, in this case.

I can see why Banksy's stencils are useful. A drawing or a painting takes five or ten minutes. With a stencil, I could be done in seconds. The nighttime concierge says hello to me as I cross the lobby toward the elevators. I barely wave in response. I'm too busy planning.

Holden's unusually quiet on the way to Saanvi's house on Monday morning. I figure he's daydreaming about a certain person's tights and high heels. He'll probably want to talk all about Miranda for the rest of the day.

It turns out I'm right. But not in the way I think.

As soon as Saanvi joins us, and we're out of sight of her house, Holden pulls up his text stream and shows us a video clip sent by one of the orangutans. The video shows Miranda rushing through the hallway. Someone sticks out a foot—accidentally or on purpose, it's impossible to tell— and she goes sailing over it. Her books fly into the air, her pencil case slides down the hall, and she lands hard on her elbows and her chin. The video plays her fall forward, then in reverse, then forward again, like an internet GIF.

It's a little different than the others. It looks as if it were shot on someone's phone, not stolen from the school cameras. And it's been texted directly to Holden.

I lean closer to read the words below the video.

YOU IN OR OUT, BRO? THESE THREE POINTS PUT JOSH IN THE LEAD.

Saanvi and I have stopped walking.

"It's your fault I'm involved in this," Holden says.

Saanvi nods, her nose wrinkled like she's smelled something rotten. "Seriously, completely, horribly our fault."

Ugh. If I felt icky looking at poor Marcus's fly video last week, or Ana's nose-picking, I feel a thousand times worse now. Maybe if I'd caused more of a stink about my video—if I'd told Mom and George, and let them call meetings and raise hell—this new clip wouldn't exist.

Thinking about Marcus reminds me. "Hey, have either of you seen Marcus lately?"

They both shrug.

"I think he found out about his video and then quit school or something. I haven't seen him in ages."

"That's terrible," Saanvi says.

"But we have a bigger issue here," Holden says, waving his phone at us.

"Tell Josh you're out," I say. "Then it's done."

"No, don't," Saanvi says. She's peering closely at the screen, zooming in on the video.

"What do you mean, no?" Holden says.

"If you say no, we lose our access to what they're planning."

Holden looks as disgusted as I feel. I can't really blame him. The guy avoids group work like the plague for three years, and then we rope him into a demented sort of project with a group of primates.

"Saanvi, we can't make him participate. If these guys are caught, they'll get expelled."

"How would they get caught? They can't post on the forums anymore. Now they're just sending videos to their own group. No one's going to rat them out. And even if they did get caught, they wouldn't be expelled. Not with Josh in the lead."

"Exactly. Josh wouldn't get expelled, so they'd need a scapegoat," Holden says miserably.

"This video isn't an accident. It's well planned. I want to see where they shot it." With that, Saanvi hitches up her backpack and starts fast-walking toward the school.

"You are not sucking me into this!" Holden shouts, hurrying to catch up.

They argue the rest of the way, and continue in whisper-hisses as they cross the foyer.

Then Saanvi stops abruptly, her eyes on the alcove.

"What *is* that?" She pulls out her phone. "What's a *panopcon*?"

I bite my tongue before I correct her pronunciation, but that doesn't stop Holden from glancing my way.

"The squirrel's an interesting choice," he says.

I make a noncommittal sound. I've been wanting to tell

them, but now I've forgotten everything I planned to say. I've forgotten how I was planning to explain the connection between graffiti squirrels and our security system issues.

"A panopcon's a prison of some sort," Saanvi reads from her phone. She's still mispronouncing it, and it kills me not to say the word properly.

I'm literally saved by the bell.

Saanvi points as the three of us hurry toward homeroom.

"This is where Miranda's video was shot. In this hallway. And look. That's Josh's locker, right there."

"Looking for me?"

Ugh. That voice. As soon as I hear it, my shoulders tense.

"It's really impressive," Saanvi says.

"What?"

"That you can still form words, when your IQ's so low."

She says it loudly enough for his friends to hear, and there's a chorus of hoots and comebacks until Max throws a basketball at Josh's head.

"Stop playing around, man. We're going to be late."

They duck into the classroom. Max glances over his shoulder and it's possible he gives me the tiniest of nods. It's also possible I'm imagining things.

Saanvi swears quietly as we drop into our homeroom desks. "I am SO going to get him extra expelled."

Holden points out that being expelled is like being dead. You can't be extra dead. Since I'm smarter than Holden, I keep my mouth shut through attendance. Ms. Marcie reads

117

the announcements, going on forever about the school's annual open house on May 15, and Mitchell Academy's "exhibition of student achievements." We're all invited to participate.

"How tempting." Holden yawns.

When the bell rings, Saanvi heads for math while Holden and I climb the stairs toward ethics.

Ana appears beside Holden, her legs taking two steps for each one of his. "Did you hear the announcement? I *love* the open house. What are you going to submit?"

She loves the open house? I have to admit, I've never been to it. It's more of a fundraising event for parents and alumni.

"I'm going to stay home and scrape my eyes out with a spoon," Holden says.

Ana looks horrified.

"But you're coming, right, Dommie?"

I almost laugh. Her eyes are so wide, she looks like a doll I used to have. When I put it down in its crib, its eyes closed. When I stood it up, they fluttered open.

"Oh, I'm definitely coming. I think I'm going to create a life-sized sculpture as my submission. Or maybe a mural across the entire school entrance."

"I think you might need special permission." She looks sincerely concerned, and I feel a little guilty.

"I'm kidding, Ana. I don't think I'm going."

"But . . ."

I peel off toward my desk and I don't hear the rest of her sentence. I *do* notice Miranda, though, in the desk across from mine. Her eyes are red and puffy.

It's hard to be properly jealous when someone's that miserable.

"Sorry," I whisper, sliding into my seat. "It gets easier after a few days."

"Don't let them see you sweat," Holden says, settling into the desk in front of hers.

She sniffs and nods. Then Ms. Sutton breezes into class and we get to forget about cameras for a while.

Ahead of Her Time
Dominica Rivers

Though barred from art school because of her gender, Montreal painter Henrietta Edwards studied privately in New York under portrait artist Wyatt Eaton. Her paintings of public figures such as Wilfrid Laurier and Lord Strathcona were exhibited widely. But Henrietta was just as dedicated to her work for equal rights. She and her sister ran a progressive women's magazine, established an organization to provide girls with housing and jobs, and embarked on a private study of women's rights laws. Henrietta went on to help women win the right to vote.

I can't very well hand in my Banksy proposal while I'm planning my own acts of graffiti. That would be like putting a guilty sticker on my forehead. Besides, I can't find my Banksy notes in my binder. I dredge up a memory from one of George's past book loans, and I scribble a new project proposal in five minutes flat.

My next class is art, a nice escape from the drama of the rest of the school. Except that Ms. Crofton is still wearing her baggy clothes, and Marcus is still missing.

I don't know where Miranda's supposed to be during second period, but she apparently isn't doing schoolwork. A blog notification pops up in the middle of class. I slide my phone beneath my desk to read it.

The Mitch Mash
Security Scandal Simmering
by Miranda Bowen

Another inappropriate school video has surfaced, this one showing a student being intentionally tripped in the hallway. That student is me.

Last week, the forums were closed after anonymous users uploaded files showing a teacher sitting on her desk, a student having a wardrobe malfunction, a student picking her nose, and another taking off her shirt. These posts were removed, but copies continue to circulate.

The original videos were obtained through school security cameras. The most recent, showing me being tripped, was filmed on a cell phone and circulated via text message. A copy was sent to me by a source who wishes to remain anonymous.

Impressive. I kind of wish I'd gone public with my video, just to show everyone I wasn't upset. Except I was upset.

And at least Miranda's not showing her bra in hers.

I slide my phone away and turn back to our perspective exercise, drawing a city street stretching into the distance. I'm filling in the lampposts when Ms. Crofton stops by my desk.

"This is nice shading," she says, touching the paper gently.

"Saanvi and I take after-school lessons on Fridays," I say.

"We've been working on shading." For weeks now, because Andrei is obsessed.

"Well, keep up the good work," she says.

"Ms. Crofton," I blurt before she can move away. "Did you talk to Marcus?"

She looks uncomfortable.

"I was just worried, because he hasn't been at school since . . ."

"Well, we all deal with things in our own ways, in our own time," she says. "Hopefully he'll be back soon."

But she doesn't sound especially hopeful.

As we finish our sketches, Ms. Crofton begins lining up spray-paint cans atop the bookshelf in the back corner of the room. They must be for the next class. But they're tempting, sitting there.

It's ridiculously easy. When the bell rings, someone stops to ask Ms. Crofton a question. Everyone else is pushing toward the hallway. I pretend I'm still stuffing my laptop into my open pack as I head for the door. It takes only a nanosecond to pull a spray can from the shelf and tuck it into my bag.

CHAPTER ELEVEN
SHADOWS AND (RED) LIGHT

THE PHONE RINGS on Monday night. I know it's George, because she's the only one who ever calls our landline.

"Is your mother out tonight, darling? I could come over, and we might watch a movie together."

I've been sitting on the couch scrolling through my texts. Holden sent me Miranda's video. I watched it, and then my own library striptease, and ended up feeling more confused and angry than ever. I should have been able to prevent this. I could have kept my clothes on, for one thing. And maybe I could have stopped the videos before Miranda's was posted.

I don't think I can sit on the couch beside George and pretend that everything's normal. Not tonight.

"That's so sweet, George, but I'm exhausted and I have a ton of homework. Could we watch a movie another time?"

"Are you feeling okay? You sound stuffy."

"Maybe I'm getting a cold."

"Do you want me to bring you some soup? They have that amazing broth at the shop down the street. Soup-er, it's called. Isn't that clever?"

"I'm totally fine, George. I'm going to get my homework done and go to bed early."

"Okay, darling. Call me tomorrow and let me know how you feel."

She's going to make me cry.

"I will." I manage to sound almost normal.

"Love you," she says.

I barely get off the phone before I lose it. If there are drones peering in through the apartment building windows tonight, they're going to see snot. A lot of snot.

After a while, I climb into bed. In the dark, I can imagine my next squirrel. Though I haven't managed to tell Holden and Saanvi yet, I'm still going to paint it. It'll be bigger than the others. Much more complicated. But perfect. So perfect, I can't sleep. Eventually, I climb out of bed and spend an hour clipping a stencil out of computer paper. Cutting is trickier than drawing. It takes me seven tries to get it right. Finally, I roll it up, tuck it into my pack, and climb back into bed.

When I glance at my phone, there's a text waiting.

HOLDEN: Did you know there's a difference between hot chocolate and hot cocoa?

ME: ??

HOLDEN: One's made with milk and one with water.

ME: Which is which?

HOLDEN: Sry, no time to discuss. Busy adjusting my whole worldview.

ME: It's late! Go to bed!

Mr. Nowak drones on about variables on Tuesday morning, and I can't sit still. As soon as he turns to the whiteboard, I grab the bathroom pass and duck into the hall.

The bathroom *is* my first stop, and I tug on my hoodie while I'm in there. When Saanvi pointed out where Josh and his cretins shot the Miranda video, I remembered the blind spot outside the door of the photography lab. But if I'm wrong about the camera range, and I'm caught on video, I don't want to be easy to identify. Head down, hood pulled tight, I slide from the door of the bathroom and down the right side of the hallway, where I should be safe.

My footsteps echo.

I'm holding my stencil rolled in my hand. I have to force my fingers loose, so I don't crush it.

I'm almost to the perfect spot when I hear voices. Teachers' voices, coming around the corner.

I dive into the darkroom.

"What the—" A voice cuts through the darkness.

My heart stops.

"Dude, you can't come in when the red light is on!"

I had no idea people used this place. Who still develops film? But there are clotheslines crisscrossing the room with white prints fluttering from them. Someone's whipping them down, one after another.

The teachers' voices pass, not pausing.

I squint to see who's here in the darkness with me. I feel as if I've been caught. But I haven't done anything. Not yet.

"Dominica?"

A red light finds me, pinning me against the door.

I finally recognize the voice. It's Max. I'd forgotten he was a photographer of the old-fashioned, develop-your-own-film type. His sports shots are always in the school newspaper—slam dunks and volleyball spikes. But in here, pinned to one end of the clothesline, is a portrait of some sort.

Dropping the light from my eyes, he pulls down the photo and puts it with a stack of others.

"You could have ruined my film, dude."

"Sorry," I manage. My mouth is dry and the chemical smell makes it worse.

"What are you doing in here, anyway?"

I should go back to class. After all, Max has seen me. When the stencil appears on the wall outside, he'll tell the rest of the guys that it was me. Plus my shirt is stuck to my back with sweat and my hands are shaking. How am I even going to hold the marker?

The spray can I swiped from the art room is still in my pack. Paint will be faster.

"Are you okay?" Max asks.

I remind myself he's one of the orangutans.

"I'm fine." I should go. I fumble for the door handle in the dim light.

"Sorry about the whole video thing," he says. "I wanted to tell you that last week, but I thought talking about it might make it worse."

He sounds sincere. I pause at the door.

"So, Dom . . . what are you doing in here?"

"Kind of hiding."

"Okay . . ."

When I don't say anything else, he waves me over. "Come and look at this."

It's a picture of the side wall of The Mitch, with part of a cherry tree framed along the edge. Max has caught a gust of cherry blossoms blowing horizontally along the wall.

"It's gorgeous," I say. "Did you just happen to see them?"

"I noticed a bunch of them blowing, but I missed the shot, and then I sat outside for an hour waiting for it to happen again."

I'm taken aback. I'm going to have to rethink Max's entire personality.

"So," he says, after I've stared at his photo for a moment too long. "You're hiding."

"I'm about to paint something on the wall outside."

I don't know why I tell him. Why in the world would I blab to Max Lin when I haven't even managed to tell Holden and Saanvi? It's something about the blossoms. Or his voice in the darkroom. Or maybe the chemicals have addled my brain.

He laughs, and then he stops. "You're what? Not really?"

When I shrug, he flicks on another light. We're bathed in a weird, alien red, but at least I can see his face.

"You don't seem like the vandalism type," he says.

"It's . . . um . . . street art?" It sounds too much like a justification in front of a jury. Max isn't the judge here. I hope. I repeat the words without the question mark attached. "It's street art. I have a good reason."

"Okay . . ."

I wipe my palms on my jeans and turn to go.

"Well, good luck, dude," he says.

I crack open the door, listening for anyone in the hallway.

"Maybe you could decide soon? I have another roll of film and I don't want you wrecking it."

"Right. Sorry."

Then I think of another problem.

"Hey, Max, slam the door when you leave, and head toward math."

I don't want him blamed, and hopefully the door slamming will help. They'll have him on video heading toward the darkroom. Then they'll hear the door and see him leaving afterwards. It's not much of an alibi, with the blind spot, but it's better than nothing.

Max definitely thinks I'm crazy.

"It's important," I say.

"Sure."

Okay. Before I lose my nerve again, I take a deep breath and step into the hallway. Almost there. I glance through the door to the main photography lab. Empty. There are cameras directly above me, pointing east along the hall, but none are aimed down to where I stand. I hope.

My phone buzzes and I almost have a stroke.

It's Mom. If I don't answer, she'll start phoning.

MOM: Your room looks like a tsunami struck. Are you alright?

ME: Sorry. School project.

MOM: What kind of school project? An origami festival?

ME: I'll clean it up tonight.

MOM: My genes are catching up to you. You sure you're okay?

ME: All good. Sorry about the mess.

MOM: 😘

MOM: Working again tonight. George will pick you up for dinner.

ME: Perfect.

I'm sure I'll be great company at dinner, as I worry about getting arrested.

First things first. I glance up and down the hallway to make sure it's still empty and that I'm in the exact blind spot between the cameras. Then I pull the stencil from my bag and unroll it. Taping it as high as I can reach along the wall, I spray the paint back and forth over the paper.

It's done.

When I rip off the stencil, the art looks even bigger and bolder than I expected.

I'm still admiring it when the bell rings to change classes. Frantically, I re-roll the stencil around the paint can. I check my hood one last time, duck my head, and join the crowd emerging from the nearby art room.

I make one quick stop in the restroom and bury my paint can in the garbage.

Nothing to see here.

I feel as if I've run a marathon by the time I reach my house after school.

"Survived another day?" Lou asks as I walk through the lobby.

"Barely."

I throw my backpack into my closet, change my sweatshirt for a sundress, and brush my hair. Then I head back downstairs. George has already pulled up to the curb outside.

"How was school? Busy?" she asks.

I smooth my hair again.

"Yup. Fairly busy." All of a sudden, I feel giddy. Maybe this is why people rob banks. Maybe it's for the rush afterwards. I could be headed for a life of crime . . .

"Are you okay?" she asks, as she points the car toward Granville.

I realize I'm laughing out loud. I may be hysterical.

Get it together, Dominica.

"It was a fun day. I helped a friend with . . . um . . . a photography project."

"Holden?"

"Um . . . yes."

I am definitely the worst criminal ever. I can't even keep my lies realistic.

George clicks her tongue. "Those teachers ask a lot of you. Are you feeling alright? You look flushed."

"I'm feeling perfect."

I am. Despite my inability to construct a half-believable alibi, I'm feeling perfect. At this exact moment, I don't even care if I get caught. I've done something. I've said what I needed to say.

George parks in front of La Patisserie.

"Might as well keep it simple tonight," she says.

She orders miso-marinated sablefish. I ask for linguini. Then I manage to get my brain working for long enough to ask about her afternoon (meeting with a new artist) and her plans for the weekend (theater show). We have a delicious dinner, including a slice of tiramisu, which we share.

"Oh, I almost forgot. I brought you a book," George says, as we're finishing the last bites.

"I kinda want to keep the Banksy one for a little longer. Is that alright? Do you need it back in the gallery store?"

She waves a hand. "No, no. Keep it as long as you want. I ordered this one specially for you, to go with it."

It's a thick hardcover with a sort of academic look. *Reclaiming the Streets: A History of Urban Art*.

"Not that I'm encouraging you to go spray-painting things, of course."

I nearly choke. "Of course."

"But I thought it would make a nice companion to the other book."

"I love it."

She beams at me. It's really not difficult to make George happy.

It's not until she's dropped me back at the apartment and I'm changing into my pajamas that I notice the black patch of paint on my finger.

I scrub at it under the bathroom sink. I scrub it with soap, and then with bathtub cleanser, and it still doesn't come off.

I wonder if Banksy ever had this problem.

The apartment seems too quiet. When I've finished my homework, I search Graydon Cameron again and spend a while imagining what it might have been like to live with him.

George says he was wild, and Mom was wild, and she didn't settle down until after his death.

Years ago, when Mom was working and I was mad about getting left at home with a babysitter, I used to imagine my dad had faked his own death. He'd arrive in a limousine to tell me he'd been living in Costa Rica the whole time. He'd come back to collect me.

"Come and stay with me," he'd say.

"What about Mom?"

"There will be a custody dispute." He'd nod mysteriously.

Custody dispute. Those were the words I'd learned from Mom after that little boy disappeared from our neighborhood. *Missing: Daniel Donavan.* His sad eyes looking out from beneath long lashes. When they found him, Mom said it had all been a custody dispute.

Probably, the custody dispute would make my dad want to whisk me all the way to Costa Rica, where I'd learn to surf and speak sign language with monkeys. Mom would have to put up posters and tell everyone I was missing. Then she'd be sorry for leaving me with the babysitter.

I shake my head at the memory of my custody dispute fantasy. I suppose I was a little confused about kidnappings. And maybe limousines, too.

Graydon Cameron does have nice eyes, though. They crinkle at the corners when he laughs. I'm not sure how I feel about Google preserving him forever, but at least he looks happy in the photos.

I meet Holden and Saanvi for milkshakes after school on Wednesday. Saanvi's fine when we arrive, and fine when I leave for the bathroom and Holden goes to pick up our fries at the counter. But she reads Miranda's latest blog post while we're gone, and then . . .

She's spitting mad. Literally. As she talks, bits of french fry fly across the table.

Holden presses himself against my shoulder to avoid the shrapnel.

"You saw this, right?" Saanvi demands, shaking her phone at me.

The Mitch Mash
Opinion: Administration Ignoring Cyberspace
by Miranda Bowen

As each day passes, I worry that Mitchell Academy is showing a dangerous lack of concern regarding cybersecurity and the well-being of students. One student appears to have left the school entirely after a cyberbullying incident in which a photo of his open fly was posted on the school forums. Other students seem too upset to speak publicly about disparaging photos and videos.

While Principal Plante has hired a private security firm, it's unclear whether the company's mandate is to protect students or to monitor them. On being confronted with a list of online issues, Ms. Plante promised to consider the matter further, but also suggested that I "grow a thicker skin."

I scowl. "Yes, I read it."

"'Grow a thicker skin!' Can you believe Ms. Plante said that?"

Holden and I obediently shake our heads.

I was just as furious as Saanvi when I read the blog post an hour ago. But I feel a bit better now that I have a plan in mind. A way to express my own opinions about all of this.

"This is ridiculous. We have to do something," Saanvi says.

I think there's french fry in my hair. It seems disrespectful to check right now, though.

"I was thinking . . . ," I start.

Holden looks at me expectantly.

"Force the school to launch a full-scale investigation into the videos," Saanvi rages. "Miranda's right. This is cyberbullying. We should write a press release. You do that part, Dom. We can go to the media."

"Or, we could do something completely different," Holden says. "Right, Dom?"

He gives me a strange look.

"Media coverage—" Saanvi starts.

"Miranda's mom is a real news person. If the news was interested, don't you think she would have done the story already?" Holden says.

I nod quickly.

"We'll have to *make* them interested," Saanvi insists.

"How?"

"We'll start a petition. Then hold a protest."

"You're kind of terrifying this afternoon," Holden tells her.

"I just want to DO something. Something big! We can't let the school get away with this."

Now I picture myself with a clipboard, standing under one of Ms. Plante's cameras, explaining to people why we need an official investigation into Josh, Max, and company. Ms. Plante is stalking toward me, high heels clacking on the vinyl. This sounds terrible.

"Tell me you don't still think this will stop on its own," Saanvi demands, waving a fry at us.

"Of course not," I say.

Holden's staring at me again.

"What?" I demand. "Stop looking at me like that."

I can't blurt out everything under these circumstances. Saanvi's practically yelling, there are tons of people around us, and . . . well . . . I still haven't figured out how to make squirrels sound powerful.

"Can you guys pay attention?" Saanvi says. "I'm going to do something about this. You know what? I'm going to call a school-wide meeting."

"A meeting?" Holden says doubtfully.

"Everyone should be consulted. Everyone. You two can . . ."

"No," Holden says.

I bite my tongue and wait for the crossfire, which is about to happen because Saanvi's slowly turning a scary shade of burnt sienna.

"Holden, you absolutely cannot keep saying this will—"

"Hang on," Holden says. He's focused on his phone.

When he looks up, he's gone pale. Flake white.

"Max sent a new video," he says. "None of the guys made it, Max says."

Saanvi grabs the phone, sets it between us on the table, and presses Replay.

Classical violin music sounds in the background as shots of Saanvi and Holden flip past. Holden and Saanvi together in the library. Holden and Saanvi across from one another in the cafeteria. Holden and Saanvi on the street near their houses. She's hanging onto his elbow, laughing.

It's not the images themselves that make me bite the inside of my lip. It's Saanvi. It's the look on her face.

In every single shot, she's staring at him. She might as well have the word CRUSH in neon-pink letters on her forehead. No, worse than that. LOVE. And Holden's smiling back at her.

I'm in the pictures, too, in the background. I'm like the wallpaper.

I stare at the phone. I'm sure I'm alizarin crimson and quinacridone magenta and yellow ochre all swirled together in one hideous palette.

"It's stupid," Holden says. "The way they've edited everything to make it seem like . . ."

I flick a finger at the screen to scroll up. PixSnappy. The entire montage is posted on the school's official PixSnappy account.

Saanvi scrapes her chair back, grabs her pack, and walks out of the restaurant.

Holden and I stare at one another for a minute, then we scramble after her.

"It's like on those reality shows," Holden gasps as we run down the street. How did Saanvi get so far, so fast?

"They can make it look like anything they want is happening." He sounds hopeful.

"They can," I agree.

"So this isn't true at all. They made it up."

"If you say so."

As we gain on Saanvi, she spins around. "Guys, I need a few minutes to cool down. I'll text you."

We putter to a stop, as if our batteries have run out of juice. Then we watch her stride to the corner and disappear.

I understand. I want to disappear, too. Teleport myself back to my room and pull the covers over my head.

I'm still holding Holden's phone. I hand it back.

"I'd better get home."

"Wait!" Holden turns with me and keeps pace. "We can fix this. We'll talk to Principal Plante again and she'll—"

"She'll say we should all grow thicker skins."

I can't quite look at him.

He knows. He knows I like him. That I've liked him for years. How could he possibly have missed it? And I've always thought he was into me, too, but neither of us was quite ready to take that final step of changing a carefully balanced friendship triangle into . . . something else. Even though it bothered me when he flirted with Miranda, I knew, deep inside, that was nothing serious. Miranda flirts with everyone. But maybe all this time, Saanvi's liked Holden, too. And he's known that she's liked him. And she's probably known that I like him. And everything I thought about the three of us was wrong and skewed and completely naive.

I feel like an idiot.

As we get close to my apartment building, Holden touches my arm.

"Can we talk about this? Before . . ." He can't look at me either. He's staring at the pavement near my toes.

"It's no big deal. I'm sorry you got sucked into all of this, though. You have your very own video now." My voice is impressively steady. I sound almost nonchalant. Almost.

"Dom," Holden says. His voice crackles. "I know that we . . ." He trails off.

My face is burning. I might melt into a molten lava puddle of embarrassment.

"I have to go," I tell him. "We'll figure things out tomorrow."

I turn so quickly that an old lady on the sidewalk has to dodge around me. A moment later, I'm leaning against the mirrored wall of the elevator, thankful for the silence.

I told Holden we'd figure things out tomorrow, but I don't want to. I may not ever want to talk about this. Ever.

I'd like to think about squirrels. More squirrels. That seems safe.

The piece I painted after leaving the darkroom is bigger than any of the others. Big enough that Ms. Plante won't be able to ignore it. I wonder if she might suspect Saanvi, because of this video. At least Saanvi won't have to lie about her innocence.

Though she seems fairly practiced at lying.

I'm going to think about squirrels.

CHAPTER TWELVE
TRUE LOVE?

DESPITE DECIDING to never again watch the video, I do. And then I watch it again. And maybe one more time on Thursday morning. Or five. Maybe six or seven more times.

I watch it often enough to be sure that Saanvi really is looking at Holden in that way. What I can't decide is whether he's looking back.

There should be online guides for this. Why have they developed facial recognition if the computer can't tell you which look means what?

Eventually, I pack my stuff and head to school early. It's either that or stare at my phone until my brain explodes.

ME: Going to school early. See you in homeroom.

HOLDEN: Wait for me. Brt.

ME: No need.

HOLDEN: It's no problem.

ME: I'll see you at school.

It's weird to be in the hallways by myself. They're so empty. If my footsteps weren't echoing, I'd feel invisible. Maybe I'm meant to be invisible.

Anonymous.

No one's noticed my work from yesterday. I suppose it's above eye-level, high up near the camera. Don't people ever look up?

I passed Max in the hallway after school yesterday and he raised his eyebrows. I think he was asking if anyone had seen it. If I'd heard anything.

I shook my head. Nothing.

I suppose it could take days. Banksy often waits a long time for people to notice his work. I read about it in the new book from George.

In 2005, someone wandered into the British Museum in London. He was dressed in an old man's trench coat, hat, and scarf. Maybe the man carried a small red gift bag, the kind in which you might bring chocolates to a friend.

For a while, he strolled through the galleries, not looking at much. Not talking to anyone.

In a room of medieval artifacts, he paused. Maybe the room was empty. Maybe there were people present, their eyes glued to other works, paying no attention to the old man.

No one knows, because there were no cameras. Not pointing in that direction, at least.

The man glued a small, painted rock to the wall. It showed a caveman pushing a shopping cart.

Below, he placed a white card that matched the others in the gallery. It read:

Early man venturing toward the out-of-town hunting grounds
This finly preserved example of primitive art dates from the Post-Catatonic era. The artist responsible is known to have created a substantial body of work across South East of England under the moniker Banksymus Maximus but little else is known about him. Most art of this type has unfortunately not survived. The majority is destroyed by zealous municipal officials who fail to recognise the artistic merit and historical value of daubing on walls.

No one noticed the rock for three days. And it was only found then because a museum worker happened to see Banksy's website, where there was a challenge to find his hoax within the museum.

The British Museum kept his art.

I wish I had Banksy's level of courage.

When I arrived at school this morning, I scanned my ID tag. Ms. Plante will know I was here early, so it's too risky to add any squirrels to my collection. I'm not quite sure what to do with myself. I don't want to go to homeroom—Mr. Nowak might be there already. I decide to aim for the library instead. I've never even considered that they might have a book about Banksy. It's a long shot, but maybe I'll check.

The library's closed.

School hours only, a sign reads, *due to staffing shortages.*

Please speak with your teachers about appropriate times to exchange books.

Great.

I'm turning away when I see it.

A squirrel. No, not a squirrel. A groundhog? It's a badly drawn blob of an animal along the wall at the base of the library doors, and it's holding a protest sign that reads, simply, "Resist."

Someone else has painted street art! Or school art, I suppose.

I'm in love.

I clap my hand over my mouth before I can laugh out loud. Then I quickly glance up and down the hallway. There's a camera pointed directly at me.

With one last glance at the groundhog (marmot?), I scurry away. But I'm much happier with the world than I was ten minutes ago.

GEORGE: Got the ding! You were certainly prompt this morning. Already at school?

ME: Early bird and all that . . .

GEORGE: Have a lovely day, darling.

I walk slowly through the school, dodging groups of kids as they arrive. I'm looking for new spots to tag. I feel as if the marmot (chipmunk?) needs company. But where should I paint next? The girls' bathroom? The boys'? Those are surveillance-free zones. And I know there aren't cameras in the locker rooms.

I'm turning into a criminal.

I have to stop myself from smiling again.

I find a few more blind spots. There's the one at the base of the stairs between the science labs. There might be another near the door to the resource room.

The hallways get too crowded before I decide for sure. It's hard to properly assess wall space when people's backpacks are bumping me and sixth graders are kicking a sandwich across the floor.

I turn toward homeroom. As I get close, I find Ana taping a poster to the wall.

"You draw, right?" Ana says. "It's not too late to submit your work! I could help you get it ready if you wanted. You know, help you choose the best pieces . . ."

"Um . . . that's okay. Thanks, though."

"There's tons of people there. Someone really important might see your work."

"I'll think about it."

Which I won't, of course, but I'm eager to escape because I can hear Saanvi's voice.

I peek around the corner of the hall to find her standing in an alcove, pointing a finger threateningly toward Josh. I don't know how she caught him without his sidekicks.

"You posted that video of Dom," Saanvi says. "And now there's a video of me on PixSnappy." Her voice is impressively level.

Josh is playing with his phone and he doesn't bother looking up from the screen. "You have no way of knowing I posted anything."

Mitchell Academy's
ANNUAL
OPEN HOUSE

WEDNESDAY, MAY 15TH, 6 P.M.

This is our school's fundraising event of
the year, and your opportunity to impress.
Apply now to submit your work for our
Gallery of Student Achievement!

Securitas genera victoria!

Maybe Saanvi and I have some things to talk about, and maybe I was avoiding her this morning. But that doesn't even remotely mean I'm leaving her to deal with Josh alone.

"Actually, she does," I say, stepping forward to block the entrance to the alcove.

"We accessed the forum logs after Dom's video and we found your name, the time of posting . . . everything," Saanvi says.

"You accessed the logs? Isn't that sort of against the rules?" Josh crosses his arms and leans against the plaster wall. He seems entirely unconcerned.

"Against the rules? Kind of like invading people's privacy? And posting obscene videos?"

"Hey, I wasn't the one who stripped in school."

"That was—" I start.

Saanvi instantly drowns me out. She calls Josh a half-dozen unkind names, the type of names I've never heard her say before.

Josh shakes his head. "Language. I'm shocked."

Her voice drops, which makes it even scarier. "The footage came from the security cameras," she says. "Which you have access to, from your mom's computer."

"Nope."

"It was posted with *your* log-in information."

This whole scene is giving me a stomachache, but I'm also bursting with pride. Saanvi is fierce.

Josh is still unmoved. "Even if I did post it, and I'm not saying I did, it didn't come from me. It was sent to me. So why don't you look for the source, rather than persecuting the innocent?"

With that, he brushes by me and into the hall.

"You are not innocent!" Saanvi yells after him.

I gape at her. "That was unbelievable."

She shakes her head. "That was kind of stupid. What good is it going to do? I was stressed about the whole . . . Holden video thing . . ."

Which makes me remember. The Holden video thing.

But this was still awesome, and I tell her so. "We can talk about the video later," I say. "And we'll figure out what to do about Josh, too."

Unfortunately, that's not quite the way it happens.

In the middle of first period, I tag the space between the science rooms. I draw two squirrels, one eating a nut, seemingly unaware, and the other holding a camera. The squirrel holding the camera has the same hair-swish as Josh, and I'm so busy silently giggling at my own private joke that I almost forget to be nervous this time.

That is, until a few minutes before lunch, when the PA crackles, and Ms. Marcie's voice echoes through our classroom.

"Excuse the interruption. Saanvi Agarwal and Dominica Rivers, please report to the principal's office."

My heart thuds against my ribs, and I stop breathing.

Did someone see me this morning? But why include Saanvi?

Maybe this is about something different. Maybe it's coincidental.

I ignore Holden's raised eyebrows. I avoid the glances from the rest of the class as I make my way toward the door. I've never been summoned to the office before. Never.

"Take your books, Dominica, in case you don't come back," Ms. Sutton calls.

I'm sure she doesn't mean to sound so ominous. Does she?

At the office, I look to Ms. Marcie for clues. Is she smiling less broadly than usual?

"Go ahead," she says.

And then Ms. Plante is waving me inside.

"Dominica. Come in. I'll just shut the door behind you."

Principal Plante's scarf today is blue with tiny yellow flecks. The fact that it's horrendously ugly doesn't help the sinking feeling in my stomach. Saanvi's already sitting on one of the chairs, her lips pressed tightly together.

"Something has come to our attention," Principal Plante says, settling herself into her giant executive's chair.

She clicks her keyboard, and Saanvi's voice spills into the room: "We accessed the forum logs after Dom's video and we found your name, the time of posting . . . everything."

I glance at Saanvi. She's turned white. Zinc white.

The principal clicks again. This time, we hear Saanvi swearing.

"Am I correct that this is your voice, Ms. Agarwal?"

Saanvi nods.

"And I believe you're on the recording as well, Ms. Rivers."

It's not a question, but I still nod. I'm sweating. I think I've had nightmares about this situation before. I feel as if I'm facing a firing squad. Maybe it's an invisible firing squad.

I'm being ridiculous.

For Josh or Max, this would be no big deal.

For Banksy, this would be no big deal.

"We expect high standards of behavior here at Mitchell

146

Academy," Principal Plante says. "Saanvi, accessing the forum logs is a serious violation. And using that sort of language to bully another student is entirely unacceptable. Not something I would have expected from you."

"She was provoked," I blurt. This is not something I expect from *me*, but even with my phobia of getting in trouble, I recognize the ridiculousness of what she's saying. Josh and his friends say much, much worse than this every ten minutes in the hallway. The idea of Saanvi bullying them is ludicrous. It's like we've been sucked through a black hole and into opposites-world.

"Normally, we would take these matters before a disciplinary board," Principal Plante continues, folding her hands on the desk. She pauses, as if she's waiting for us to speak.

"That's not . . . I don't . . ." I manage nothing coherent.

"I would prefer to deal with this in school, if possible, so it doesn't take time away from my studies," Saanvi says.

Even though I know she's lying her pants off—she doesn't care about her studies; she cares about her parents not finding out—I'm still amazed at how professional she manages to sound.

"I'll need the precise details of how you accessed the forums," Principal Plante says.

"Of course."

There's a long pause, while the principal drums her polished nails on the desk and stares at us.

"If you're willing to apologize," she says finally, "and since this is a first offense—"

"I'm certainly very sorry," Saanvi says.

"Me too."

"Perhaps a written apology to Josh, in this instance, would be more appropriate." The principal smiles tightly, as if she hadn't just kicked us in the guts with those words.

I want to disappear into the wool carpeting, but my head is nodding. It's nodding without my permission.

"I trust this won't happen again."

"It won't," Saanvi says.

"Well, then, I suppose we're done here, girls."

"Thank you, Ms. Plante."

Saanvi is still in professional mode. Is it possible she's been abducted and replaced by an alien robot version of herself?

"Thank you," I echo. Have I been replaced, too?

We leave the office, walk past Ms. Marcie without acknowledging her, and join the crush of the crowd between classes. I can't remember exactly where I'm supposed to be.

"Did we agree to write a letter of apology to Josh? Did that just happen?"

When Saanvi turns to look at me, she's not an alien robot anymore. Even though she has tears in her eyes, she manages to look spitting mad.

"I'm sorry I got you sucked into this."

"YOU'RE sorry?"

Saanvi glances down the hall, and up toward the camera. "It's going to kill me to write that letter. But she had us on tape. Josh must have recorded us. What else were we supposed to do?"

There are a lot of things I would have liked to do, if I were a completely different person. Riot, for example. Throw a massive tantrum. Flip Principal Plante's perfect desk. But none of those things is exactly in my wheelhouse. None of them would play well on camera, either.

". . . living in a surveillance state . . . ," Saanvi mutters.

It's true. If we get any more protected, The Mitch won't be a school for gifted kids. It will be a school for robots. People will be scared to talk in the halls, in case they're recorded. No one will want to discuss things in class, in case Ms. Plante's all-seeing eye lands upon them. And the people with connections—like Josh—will do or say whatever they want.

". . . there has to be a way to speak out about this . . ."

I let Saanvi ramble, my own brain still spinning. The more I think about these posts and videos, the more they begin to seem like puzzle pieces. Piece: Josh and Max are part of a contest. Piece: Josh has access to the school systems. Piece: Ana has codes in her binder. Piece: Ms. Plante is raising funds by promoting her stellar security system, "protecting" students online and in real life.

I just need to fit the puzzle pieces together.

Saanvi tugs at my sleeve and I realize I've stopped, midhallway.

"I have to get to class. I really am sorry," she says. Her teeth are ground so tightly together, the words sound muddled.

I turn back toward ethics. When I get there, everyone's doing project work. I tear a blank page out of my binder. I may as well get this over with.

Dear Josh:

Please accept my apology for this morning's incident. My friend and I were upset and unfairly took out our

149

frustrations on you. Our actions were obviously not in keeping with our school's standards. It will certainly not happen again.

Sincerely,
Dominica Rivers

When the bell rings, I drop it off with Ms. Marcie, before I can change my mind.

I can barely believe Saanvi and I agreed to write letters of apology to Josh, and then we thanked Principal Plante. We *thanked* her.

I feel like smashing this entire security-camera, PixSnappy, forum-post mess. I think I know how to do it, too.

CHAPTER THIRTEEN
MUD MASKS

MOM'S WAITING for me in the living room after school. There are two giant pizza boxes on the coffee table, one of them already open.

"Whoa."

"Vegetarian or Hawaiian?"

This isn't a good sign. Mom only gets takeout when . . .

"Did something go wrong with Frank?"

"Frank who?" she asks, through a giant bite of ham and pineapple.

I go to the kitchen for some paper towel. Then I join her on the couch and grab a piece before she eats it all. Hawaiian *is* my favorite.

"I thought we could watch a movie," Mom says. "Oooh . . . and I bought pomegranate-avocado mud masks. Tonight can be spa night!"

Whatever happened, it must have been bad.

She passes me the remote. "You choose," she says. And then, five minutes later, "Really?"

I suppose she was expecting a rom-com.

"This is supposed to be really good. Look—it has ninety-eight percent." It's a movie made by Banksy. I read about it in the book George bought me.

Mom flips open the box of vegetarian and grabs a piece. "Fine. But we get popcorn halfway through, and you make it."

"Deal."

"And we need bits of cheese sprinkled on top."

"Fine."

As it turns out, *Exit Through the Gift Shop* is 98 percent interesting and also 100 percent weird. It's about this film-maker named Thierry who idolizes graffiti artists. He ends up helping Banksy plant a fake Guantanamo-Bay prisoner inside a ride at Disneyland, a pretty amazing breach of Disney security. But then Thierry creates a film that's so messed up, it's unwatchable. Banksy distracts him with an art show and takes over the editing himself.

In the end, Thierry sells almost a million dollars of art, even though no one's actually sure if he's an artist. And the movie—in real life—gets rave reviews and wins awards, even though no one's actually sure if it's a real movie.

Mom seems fairly into it for the first little while, and I deliver the popcorn as promised. But when the credits roll and I glance her way, her cheeks are wet. There are smeared mascara circles beneath her eyes.

"Mom! We could have turned it off!"

"It's fine. It's not the movie." She wipes her nose on a scrap of paper towel.

"Okay, what did he do?"

"Who?"

"You know who! Frank!"

Reluctantly, she lifts a pizza box lid off her phone and logs into PixSnappy.

"You're on PixSnappy?"

This seems highly unfair, when I apparently have a lifetime ban.

"For work!" she says. "I only post pictures of food."

"And you stalk people," I say, once she passes me her phone.

On her screen, there's a picture of Frank with his arms around an Asian woman. She's definitely not my mother.

"I guess she's not his sister." Frank is titanium white.

Mom snorts.

"Ugh. Sorry," I say, handing her phone back to her. Poor Mom. At least I'll have her home a bit more now. Although . . .

"Avocado masks!" she says, bouncing up.

Twenty minutes later, I'm back on the couch watching the cooking channel and trying not to blink. Slowly, as the avocado hardens, new bits of my skin pucker.

"How do you know if it's working?" I mumble.

Mom shushes me. We're not supposed to move our faces for twenty minutes. After which we have to steam.

I'm not sure I can handle Mom being home all the time.

I escape to the bathroom, where I read Miranda's latest blog post.

The Mitch Mash
Going Squirrelly
by Miranda Bowen

Several squirrels (and one animal that appears to be a ferret) have taken up residence in The Mitch hallways this week. You'll find them in an alcove near the office, outside Division 8, and high above the west hallway. They're not real animals,

153

of course! They appear to have been painted or drawn in black ink.

The largest piece, in the west hall outside the photography lab, shows three squirrels bent over school desks. From one side of them, a teacher (also a squirrel) watches. On the other side, the actual Mitch security camera appears to loom over the scene. Most of the art pieces feature the words "The Panopticon," referring to a type of prison in which prisoners must live as if they're constantly watched.

So . . . with all the security at The Mitch, how did this mystery artist place his squirrels directly beneath the camera?

"The camera angle didn't cover the spot where the person was standing, dear. Only someone's hand is visible," a member of The Mitch office staff told this reporter. She has requested anonymity.

There's been a lot of talk about privacy recently, after several embarrassing photos and videos were sent by email, posted on the school forums, and shared on social media.

Saanvi Agarwal, who suggests the entire student body should be more widely consulted on technology issues, said this: "The problem is happening because our school super-values security over privacy, right? There are so, so many cameras around here. It's like a complete surveillance state."

Saanvi suggested that an outdated school code of conduct is also to blame: while we have internet-use guidelines, there are no rules regarding social media or technology.

"We need to get the cameras out of our classrooms, talk to everyone about privacy, and set seriously serious standards for social media posting," she said.

It seems the squirrels agree.

(Other squirrel sightings? Leave directions in the comments below!)

When I emerge from the bathroom, Mom gasps.

"Stop smiling! You're cracking the mask!"

I try, but it's difficult. My squirrels have definitely been noticed now. And Miranda even looked up the panopticon reference.

"Stop!"

"Okay, okay."

I force myself to look serious. If I think about the Holden and Saanvi video, instead of the squirrels, it's not that hard.

It's raining lightly on Friday morning when Holden and I pick up Saanvi. All three of us have our hoods pulled around our ears.

"Did you read Miranda's post? She quoted you," Holden says.

"Did she?" Saanvi says. "Great."

Is she blushing? That makes no sense. Her quote was perfect. My squirrels, on the other hand, were attributed to a "he," but whatever. I suppose that means I'm even more anonymous.

As we reach an intersection, I flip back my hood so I can see better. Saanvi reaches to pick a flake of something from my ear.

"Ugh. Avocado," I say.

"Dom, why is there avocado in your ear?" Holden looks as if he's scared to hear the answer.

"Face masks," Saanvi says, as if it's entirely obvious.

I nod. "My mom and Frank broke up."

They make matching sympathetic faces.

It feels strange to be walking to school with them again. Neither has mentioned the video. The three of us chat like normal, but no one touches. There's an invisible bubble of space around each of us. And not just because of the rain jackets.

Holden and Saanvi have moved on to complaining about Ms. Plante.

"Did you write your Josh apology?" Holden asks.

"Done. Though it felt like selling my soul to the devil," she says. "I wish I'd refused."

"I wonder what she would have done," I say.

"You were right when you said we need to focus on the bigger problem," Saanvi tells me.

All three of us leap back from the curb as a car passes too close, causing a mud-puddle tsunami.

"I'm going to write to the board of directors," Saanvi says.

"What?" Holden brushes off his pant leg.

"Wow," I say.

"Wow, what?" she asks.

Am I supposed to say something else? I look over at her as we cross the school grounds toward the stairs.

"I'll ask for a meeting with them. Are you going to help?" Saanvi prompts.

"Oh. Um . . . yes?"

Stand up in front of men in power suits, not to mention Ms. Plante, and discuss my bra? That sounds like the worst idea ever. But it was Saanvi who marched into the principal's office with me when my video was shared. It was Saanvi who swore at Josh on my behalf. It was also Saanvi who looked at Holden that way, and didn't tell me. You'd think she would have at least mentioned it. Still . . .

"Of course I'm going to help."

She looks relieved, and I realize she wasn't sure. She was willing to do this by herself.

"Holden?"

"I have to change," he says, outpacing us. "I'm soaked."

I have no idea whether he heard anything Saanvi said. Which leaves just me . . .

I elbow Saanvi. "If they call in guards who wrap you in a straitjacket and drag you off to an asylum, where you're force-fed antipsychotic drugs, I'll break through the bars at night and rescue you."

"Perfect," she says. Then she peels off toward math, and I head for ethics.

I'll help. I'll stand behind her and nod, or pass around handouts. But it seems unlikely the board of directors will side with Saanvi over Ms. Plante.

As George would say, there are two chances: slim and none.

Ms. Sutton's wearing a kimono jacket today, woven with orange and red flowers. It swirls around her as she paces the front of the classroom.

"Artists have a responsibility to speak about political issues. Discuss."

She does this. She veers from the usual order of things to whatever current-events question has caught her interest. And it might be fun, sometimes, to talk about these things, except—

Ana throws her hand immediately into the air. "As a social media artist myself, I feel it's my role to find beauty in the world and reflect that for others. People who are suffering can look at works of art and be uplifted and feel peaceful."

This is news to me. Ana's a social media artist? What exactly is that, anyway?

"That's ridiculous." I don't mean to say it aloud. It sneaks out of me.

The whole class swivels, and I feel my cheeks growing hot. "It's just that looking at something pretty isn't going to solve world poverty or global warming. If art's going to change things, it has to make people think."

"Now, without judging other comments—" Ms. Sutton says.

Josh leans back in his desk, crossing his heels in the aisle. "It's pointless."

I want to kick him.

"No art is going to solve global warming," he says.

"So artists have no responsibility to try?" Ms. Sutton prompts.

"They can try. And fail," he says.

He turns to high-five Max. There's a ripple of laughter.

"It's not an artist's responsibility. It's a friggin' human responsibility," Holden says. And now the whole class swivels in his direction because not only has he come close to swearing but he's SPOKEN IN CLASS. VOLUNTARILY. This has never happened before.

"Holden, perhaps you can expand on that thought?" Ms. Sutton smiles at him.

He shrugs.

Ms. Sutton calls on someone else.

"Even if art can't solve global warming, it could get people t-talk . . . t-talk . . ." The guy gets hung up on a stutter and the back row erupts in imitations.

"He's right." Miranda chimes in. "If art can spark discussions, those discussions might lead to change."

"Well," Ms. Sutton says. "Obviously we have some strong feelings about this."

Ana's hand shoots up again. "I think we can agree that my position serves as a compromise—"

"Yes, Ana," Ms. Sutton says. She sounds tired, but that may be my imagination. "Let's get back to our projects, shall we? You can spend the rest of this period on your research."

I happen to meet Miranda's eyes as I reach for my laptop. She smiles at me.

I'm so surprised, I smile back.

Then, suddenly, Ms. Sutton is standing over my desk. She slides a piece of paper toward me.

Project Proposal: Banksy's Street Art

I stop breathing. How did Ms. Sutton get this? Then I remember my race from the classroom to the bathroom that day, my binder crashing to the floor and my papers scattering.

"This is fascinating, Dominica," Ms. Sutton says. "I'm surprised you switched topics."

"Well, Mary Pratt is also—"

"Henrietta, you mean? I believe your proposal suggested you were studying Henrietta Edwards."

"Right. Henrietta Edwards." I'm losing my mind.

Ms. Sutton taps my Banksy paper. "I'd love to see more on this topic, unless there is some other reason . . . ?"

All of Saanvi's inappropriate vocabulary words are swirling through my head. Ms. Sutton knows. She knows about the squirrels. Or she suspects, at least.

"I think . . . I don't . . ." This would be a really good time to be abducted by aliens.

"Well, consider it." Ms. Sutton smiles. "And be careful, no?"

I nod silently, and she wanders away.

From across the aisle, Miranda raises her eyebrows.

I shrug. I have no idea what just happened here.

As people settle into their research, Miranda slips her phone across the aisle to me.

The Mitch Mash
Forum Fiasco
by Miranda Bowen

This content has been deemed inappropriate by school administration and removed from the site.

The Mitch Mash
Security Scandal Simmering
by Miranda Bowen

This content has been deemed inappropriate by school administration and removed from the site.

I don't know what to tell her. She was the only one brave enough to really talk about all of this and admit what happened to her. And now Ms. Plante has basically censored the blog.

"This sucks," I whisper.

She doesn't answer. I can't be sure, but I think she's fast-blinking, trying not to cry.

At the end of the day, I meet Holden and Saanvi at our lockers, and we head through the hall together. Outside the darkroom, the custodian is balanced atop a ladder. He's splashing white paint over my collection of squirrels-in-desks.

Ouch.

There's a group gathered below him.

"Oh, c'mon, do you really have to?" someone says.

"That's art, dude."

"I liked those squirrels!"

I'm unexpectedly touched. And then, something on the door of the boys' bathroom makes me stop in my tracks. It's not graffiti, it's a photo. But it's a photo of my art. Someone's taken a picture of one of the squirrels and pasted a cutout of Josh's face over top of the squirrel head.

"That is epic," Holden whispers.

"Who did this?" Saanvi wonders.

I shake my head as we leave. "I have no idea."

I think Banksy would say that art is meant to change and evolve. It's not something to be bought for millions of dollars and hung in the homes of collectors, away from real people.

In 2018, a Banksy painting called *Girl with Balloon* was sold at Sotheby's auction house in London for more than a million British pounds. The moment the sale was declared and the hammer fell, the painting whirred to life. The canvas began to drop through a shredder hidden in the bottom of the frame. While people pointed and clicked photos, Sotheby's employees rushed to remove the piece from the wall.

A video clip of the Sotheby's sale appeared on Banksy's Instagram account, and a new title for the painting was announced: *Love Is in the Bin.*

My squirrels are in the bin, apparently. But I've been thinking more and more about my new idea. My go-big idea. And when I see the poster on the bulletin board, near the exit doors, everything starts to come together.

Maybe we don't need a meeting with the board of directors. Maybe we don't need blog posts. This open house could be our canvas.

As always, Saanvi's mom gives us a ride to our art class on Friday afternoon. We've already finished our warm-up sketches when the door swings open.

"Private lesson!" Andrei barks.

Holden is standing in the doorway. Both Saanvi and I stop drawing and stare. We're supposed to be starting portraits of one another. So far, paper-Saanvi has only half an eye, but that eye looks just as surprised as I am.

Holden doesn't acknowledge us. He crosses the room toward Andrei, they have a short discussion, and then Holden hands over a check.

I'm officially stupefied. If Banksy himself appeared in our art lesson, I wouldn't be this surprised. Well, I wouldn't actually recognize him, so maybe I'd just wonder why a stranger was joining our private drawing lesson, but this . . .

Mitchell Academy's
ANNUAL
OPEN HOUSE

WEDNESDAY, MAY 15TH, 6 P.M.

This is our school's fundraising event of
the year, and your opportunity to impress.
Apply now to submit your work for our
Gallery of Student Achievement!

Securitas genera victoria!
LAST CALL
FOR ENTRIES!

"Hey," Holden says, as if he stands at the easel next to mine every Friday afternoon.

Saanvi finds her voice first. "What are you doing here?"

"We need to talk," he says.

"Here?" I really don't understand.

He reaches across the gap to grab my hand, and he looks me in the eye. "Listen, that video? It's not like that."

Saanvi shakes her head. "It's really not."

"Okay." That's all I can manage.

"You think things have been happening behind your back, things you didn't know about, and that's not true," Holden says.

"I kind of decided we were over it. Do we need to talk about it now?"

"Enough chitter-chatter," Andrei says, suddenly looming over our table. "Put zee pencils on zee paper, and draw zomezing. Anyzing."

Holden turns to him. "I'm not going to disrupt your class every week. I promise. But I need five minutes."

Andrei blinks. Then he throws his hands in the air and turns away, muttering, "Five minutes. He needs five minutes, he zays. Fine. Five minutes. What use iz art, anyvay? Always, art must vait."

"It's true. There's nothing going on behind your back," Saanvi repeats.

Except maybe they planned this talk? But no. Saanvi looked as confused as I was when Holden walked into the room.

"Now, why don't you tell us what's happening behind *our* backs?" Holden says.

My brain has a complete meltdown. I open my mouth to ask what he's talking about. Then I close my mouth because it's completely obvious what he's talking about.

He knows.

I worried that he suspected. But now . . . how to explain?

"We'll wait," he says.

Saanvi crosses her arms, a small smirk on her face.

"You *have* talked about this behind my back."

"With good reason," Saanvi says. "But I didn't know we were going to figure it out today."

From his easel, Andrei mutters something about emotional drama. He sighs loudly and leaves the room.

"There's nothing—" I start. There's already been way too long a pause, though.

Holden snorts.

"If you don't want to tell us, that's fine," Saanvi says. "But that says more about this friendship than a fake video does."

Ouch.

She's right. Besides, at this moment, I can't remember why I didn't tell them everything in the first place. I suppose because, when I started, I didn't really plan the squirrels. Plus they seemed sort of silly. I didn't want to get Holden and Saanvi in trouble. And maybe . . .

"I guess I felt like Holden was okay with the way things were, and you were planning massive protests," I tell her. "I was mad at Ms. Plante, and I was reading about Banksy, and it just . . . happened."

"The graffiti," Saanvi says.

"Street art."

"The squirrels," Holden says.

"How long have you known it was me?"

Holden shrugs. "Forever. There aren't that many people who know about the panopticon."

Saanvi reaches over and flips backwards through my sketchbook, to a comic-like drawing of a cat wearing goth gear. "It took me longer than Holden. But I recognized the way you draw."

It's true. When I look at the cat's nose and its tiny paws, there are definite squirrel similarities.

"If you knew, how come you didn't say anything?"

"We thought you'd tell us," Holden says.

"Way before this," Saanvi says.

"Well, now you know."

"And what are we going to do from here?" she asks.

It turns out she's not the only one with that question. Andrei comes back, brow furrowed. "Time for talking zee emotions is finish. Yes? Put zee pencil on zee paper and draw zee emotions."

He turns to Holden. "So you stay, but no more dizruption, yes?"

When Holden nods, I raise my eyebrows at him. He's actually joining our art class?

He shrugs. "You wouldn't believe how excited my mom was to drive me here."

"Zat is zee yes, or zee no?"

"I'm staying," Holden says.

In my portrait, Saanvi ends up looking as if she's seen a tectonic plate shift, but I take no responsibility for that. I was simply reflecting reality.

After class, the three of us walk together toward the

parking lot. Saanvi's mom is in her idling car, catching up on emails, as usual. Holden's mom stands beside her own car, waving excitedly.

"Like I said, she's really happy," he mutters.

"Hey," I call, as he walks away. "Hang on one second. I have something else planned. Something bigger. So maybe we can talk about it later? If you want to help?"

Saanvi claps her hands. "I knew it!"

"Later," Holden says.

Which is not exactly zee yes or zee no.

CHAPTER FOURTEEN
SECRET SOCIETY

I SPEND all of Saturday sketching. In fact, I completely lose track of time, and when Mom comes in late from catering a dinner, I'm still sitting on the couch with papers strewn around me.

"Whoa," she says.

"Sorry!" I grab at my sketches, shoving them into a stack and tucking them beneath my arm.

"Homework?"

"Something like that."

It's enough of an excuse. Mom's so tired she can barely drag herself to the bathroom to brush her teeth.

I don't get away quite so easily on Sunday morning.

Mom and I drive to La Patisserie together. George is already there, as always, sipping her coffee.

"Dominica, darling!" she says, as I lean to kiss her.

She turns to my mom. "Pierre says they have fresh black truffles, and they're doing *brouillade de truffes* this morning. I admit, I'm tempted."

I am not tempted, because George tricked me this way last year, and that fancy-sounding dish is actually runny scrambled eggs.

"The caramel crêpes, please," I tell Pierre when he arrives.

"Ah, les craps," he says.

I manage not to laugh because Saanvi and Holden aren't here to laugh with me. But they're going to howl when I tell them about *les craps*.

"What's new with my beautiful granddaughter?" George asks, once Pierre has gone. "Are you ready to trade books yet?"

"Not yet," I tell her.

"She can't possibly have time to read," Mom says. "She had the entire living room covered in homework last night."

"On a Saturday night? What class is this for?"

"Um . . . ethics?"

Which is not technically true, because I haven't started my ethics project . . .

". . . due?" George is saying.

"Soon?"

She nods, so my answer must have made sense.

"And your drone essay? I never asked about it last week. I was distracted by that lovely Frank."

Incidentally, I got an A on my drone project. I don't get to tell George, though, because as soon as she mentions Frank, Mom starts fussing with her napkin.

"Everything okay, Carol? Did you and Frank hit a snag?"

Mom glances my way, but I didn't tell George anything!

"Too bad," George sighs. "I thought he might be a keeper."

Which seems a little extreme. I mean, he was nice. He was dressed appropriately, if a bit formally. He certainly seemed to like Mom. And food. But is Mom supposed to base an entire relationship on that?

"I thought he stopped by on Friday," George asks.

Mom eyes her curiously. "How did you know that?"

Grandma busies herself straightening her cutlery. "Dominica must have mentioned it."

"Dominica wasn't home on Friday," Mom says.

"Art class," I confirm.

Usually, I'm the only one who seems to notice George's psychic abilities, but Mom looks suspicious this time.

"Well, it must have been a lucky guess," George says.

"He didn't stay, anyway. I had to work."

"I'm sorry you couldn't talk things out, darling."

And somehow that's enough to make Mom—my scattered, heartbroken mom—forget all about George's uncanny sleuthing abilities and go back to talking about Frank. Frank's love of red wine, Frank's pro bono work, Frank's dream of living in Paris for a year . . . but also Frank's photo on social media, hugging another woman who's apparently an ex-girlfriend in town for the weekend and the hug was friendly, only friendly, or that's what he says . . .

If it's true, I might be convinced that Frank has long-term potential. Especially if it involves all of us living in Paris for a year. But Mom's not convinced.

She and George dissect the possibilities until we're distracted by the arrival of salted caramel crêpes/craps. They are much, much better than their name.

As I take my last few bites, my phone starts buzzing. I excuse myself so I can check the text in the bathroom.

> **HOLDEN:** Please call 911. Send them to Pacific Centre.

170

ME: Haha. What is the nature of your emergency, sir?

SAANVI: Once they've saved you, send them my way. I'm at the Golden Pearl Buffet, hiding in the bathroom.

ME: I'm hiding too!

HOLDEN: I'm in the changeroom at Holt Renfrew and I can't get out. Every time I try, my mom and the clerks bring more shirts. There are 3 of them!

SAANVI: 3 shirts?

HOLDEN: 3 clerks!

SAANVI: Whoa. Like a multiheaded hydra.

ME: Do you think a fire truck or an ambulance would be more help?

HOLDEN: Send both. Send all of them. I'm going under . . .

SAANVI: My aunties just joined me in the bathroom. My cover is blown.

HOLDEN: So. Many. Shirts.

When I get back to the table, Mom and George are already gathering their things. As always, George pays the bill. The host produces my jacket and helps me into it. George kisses Mom on both cheeks.

I'm about to wave at the surveillance camera above the door when I pause.

I used to imagine I was waving to a bored security guard at the other end of that camera. Now I'm not sure who's watching. I'm no longer willing to wave.

"How did you really know about Frank's visit on Friday?" I whisper to George when it's my turn for a kiss.

She pats my arm. "A woman needs her secrets," she says.

Then she's off down the street, her rose-colored silk scarf fluttering behind her, looking like a woman who's never had a secret in her life.

We're supposed to do our math homework together after school on Monday, but Saanvi looks exhausted. She doesn't even perk up when I tell her about the crêpe/crap scene at La Patisserie.

I'm not sure if she's still tired from her family gathering yesterday, or if she's upset because Miranda's video has appeared as part of a PixSnappy mash-up. She and Miranda blocked a bunch of followers and they emailed PixSnappy, but apparently the content-review people can take days to respond.

Holden holds out his phone to show me the mash-up.

"Can you put it away?" I beg. "This whole thing makes me feel icky."

"Complicit," Saanvi says.

"What does that even mean?" he asks.

"Involved. On the side of the bad guys," Saanvi says.

"We are NOT complicit," I protest.

"Easy for you to say." Holden scowls at me. "Max and Josh are still texting me about contest entries."

"Ugh. I forgot about the contest," Saanvi says.

Which makes me sit straight up in my library chair.

"I forgot something, too."

I never told these two about Ana's binder. Maybe the contest is meaningless. Maybe the guys had nothing to do with the forums, and it was all Ana.

When I explain, Holden and Saanvi look equally skeptical.

"I can't imagine Ana posting embarrassing videos, especially when she knows what it feels like to be the target," Saanvi says. "She wouldn't do that. Would she?"

I have no idea. We've been in classes with Ana for almost three years now, but all I know about her is that she likes the tips of her pencils very, very sharp and she never colors outside the lines.

"What possible reason would she have?" Holden asks.

"Maybe it's personal."

"I need to talk to you about something else," I tell them.

"Wow. Make her spill one secret, and she can't stop," Holden says.

I stick my tongue out at him.

"Tell us," Saanvi urges.

"Well, you know how the squirrels got painted over?"

"And those chipmunk things," Saanvi says.

It's true. This morning, two more of the blob-rodents appeared near the custodian's closet. They were carrying suitcases. The text above them read: *Who said anything about safe?*

They were covered up by lunchtime.

"I need help," I tell them.

"That's kind of obvious," Holden says.

"No! I mean help with a project. I need help to paint something big, something gigantic."

"Yes."

This is the shortest sentence I've ever heard Saanvi say.

"I was thinking maybe the side of the school? Or one wall of the foyer?"

"That's a fantastically awesome idea," Saanvi says.

"You want to paint gigantic graffiti in the foyer," Holden says flatly.

"Exactly."

"What's my middle name?" he asks.

"Alexander."

"Just making sure you haven't been kidnapped and replaced by an imposter."

"Holden! I'm serious! The small pieces are failing. But I still think this kind of art could get people's attention. We need to go bigger."

"You know you hate getting in trouble, right? And this will get you suspended."

Maybe.

"I was thinking about the open house," I tell them.

Saanvi immediately gasps. "The open house! That's SO perfect."

"I know."

"You'll need to do your most enormously gigantic piece ever. It needs to have impact, so everyone will see it. Then it'll get all the parents involved."

"I know."

The idea of a crowd of people looking at something I've created gives me heart flutters that are only slightly less intense than the palpitations I get thinking about Ms. Plante. This is definitely not something I'm doing alone.

"Will you help?"

"Would we wrap wet cloths around our faces, plunge into a fire, and pull you from the burning building?" Saanvi asks.

"Um . . . I think so?"

"Obviously, of course! When do we start? And exactly how humongous are we going?" Saanvi's enthusiasm makes the table shake.

"Seriously?"

"Seriously serious," Saanvi says.

Holden hasn't said anything. When I turn to him, he's staring at the carpet the same way he stared at the shrubbery on the way to school this morning.

"You totally don't have to help. I get it."

"It's not that," he says.

"Of course he has to help!" Saanvi says. "Holden, you're in, right?"

There's a long pause. Way too long.

"No. I'm out," he says eventually.

Then he grabs his math books and leaves the library.

We both stare after him.

"He can't seriously be serious," Saanvi says.

I have no idea anymore.

We spend another half hour discussing the details of my idea. But as soon as I drop Saanvi at her house, I text Holden.

ME: Okay, spill.

HOLDEN: What?

ME: I told you about the squirrels.

HOLDEN: ??

ME: If you don't tell me what's going on, I will come to your house and tell your mom that you secretly love to play Monopoly. I'll suggest she invite our entire homeroom class for an evening of board games.

HOLDEN: Not funny.

ME: On my way . . .

HOLDEN: She says I'm switching schools.

ME: WHAT? Who? When?

HOLDEN: My mom says I'm switching schools in September.

ME: WHY WHY WHY????????

HOLDEN: She says The Mitch is failing to inspire me.

ME: 😨

ME: So that's it? She's pulling you? No warning?

HOLDEN: I kind of had warning. My other choice was to join three extracurricular activities this term. Minimum.

ME: Whoa.

HOLDEN: I know. Do three separate extracurricular activities even exist?

ME: Um . . . yeah?

ME: What about the art class?

HOLDEN: That counts, but not enough.

ME: Crêpe.

HOLDEN: I know.

HOLDEN: Anyway, sorry to be a downer. I'll figure it out.

ME: ♥

ME: Saanvi and I won't let you go. We'll tie you to your desk.

HOLDEN: Perfect. That will solve everything.

A notification dings, distracting me from the texts. It's another blog post from Miranda . . . sort of.

The Mitch Mash
On Hiatus
by Miranda Bowen

After three *Mitch Mash* articles were needlessly censored by school administrators, the editors have decided to take a publishing hiatus. We will be communicating our views on other platforms. Watch for us.

Mom's things are in the hallway when I arrive home, and I sigh. We've spent a *lot* of time together lately, and I'm not sure I can eat another bite of takeout chow mein or watch one more romance.

But then . . . I think I smell something cooking. Sure enough, once I've hung Mom's purse and straightened her shoes, I find her in the kitchen with a mixing bowl and a pastry blender.

"Quiche for dinner. What do you think?"

"Yum?"

"My arms are tired. Want to cut in this butter for me?"

I take over the mixing, but I keep an eye on Mom. She seems . . . brighter.

"Did you and Frank talk today?"

"We met for lunch." She grins, looking a little guilty. "I might have jumped to conclusions about the photo."

"Not an ex-girlfriend?"

"Oh, she was, but from years ago. She has a husband and two kids, and she lives in New York. She was visiting."

Which doesn't necessarily mean he's innocent, but . . .

"He added my fingerprint to his phone. So I can check his texts if I want. Not that I'd want to, but it was a sweet gesture."

I laugh, shaking my head. "Very romantic."

She sticks out her tongue at me. "We're going out for drinks tonight. Do you mind?"

"Nope."

As it happens, I have a lot to do. Though I don't get far before Holden starts texting.

HOLDEN: I've been thinking about the logistics, and you're going to need a team to pull this off. Like in *Ocean's 11*.

SAANVI: I think he means *Ocean's 8*.

ME: I thought you weren't helping.

HOLDEN: I'm not. Because I am NOT going to be the guy who's duped into holding the diamonds.

SAANVI: That's what you think! Muahahahaha.

ME: Holden's right, but we have a team. Or we would, with the three of us.

HOLDEN: Um . . . did you just say HOLDEN'S RIGHT??? I'm taking a screenshot.

ME: What kind of criminal are you? Don't screenshot anything.

SAANVI: And about the team thing . . .

ME: I've already mapped the cameras. What else do we need?

HOLDEN: A lookout.

SAANVI: You'd make an excellent lookout.

HOLDEN: It's my innocent eyes.

SAANVI: Is that a yes?

HOLDEN: Can't.

SAANVI: Oh, for crêpe's sake.

ME: You need extracurricular activities.

HOLDEN: Yeah. This is not exactly what my mom has in mind.

SAANVI: So . . . lookout?

HOLDEN: We'll figure something out.

SAANVI: What about Miranda?

HOLDEN: What is it with you and Miranda, hmmmm????

ME: Why Miranda?

SAANVI: She can be the lookout, and she can handle communications. That's where your first plan failed. She has a thousand PixSnappy followers, and her mom's got a gazillion. You know her mom's the VTV news anchor, right?

HOLDEN: Good point. Miranda's in.

ME: Ugh. Fine.

HOLDEN: Ana?

ME: NO!

SAANVI: NO!

HOLDEN: Kidding.

ME: Four is enough. Come over tmrw afternoon and we'll figure things out.

HOLDEN: Three. I can't come.

ME: Argh.

SAANVI: Wait! One last thing.

HOLDEN: ?

SAANVI: I don't want to be a team.

ME: ???

SAANVI: I'm thinking . . . secret society.

ME: Seriously?

HOLDEN: Seriously?

SAANVI: So much more romantical!

ME: Fine. We're a secret society. See you tomorrow.

HOLDEN: You should probably have a secret handshake.

ME: 😊

CHAPTER FIFTEEN
TRESPASSING AND TREASON

WHEN SAANVI and I get to the apartment after school on Tuesday, Mom pulls a tray of triple-chocolate brownies from the freezer. Which is amazing, because the only thing better than triple-chocolate brownies is frozen triple-chocolate brownies.

"If we'd told Holden there would be brownies, he might have come," Saanvi says.

"Is he not coming? That's too bad," Mom says. I try to shoo her away, but she ignores me. She's still hovering a few minutes later, when Miranda buzzes up.

"Sorry I'm late," she says, slipping off her high heels.

I reluctantly introduce her to Mom.

"Wow. I can see where Dom gets her bone structure. You have the most amazing cheekbones," Miranda says.

Mom touches her cheeks, as if realizing for the first time she has bones there. "Do I?"

"I always notice, because my family works in television. You'd be great on camera."

And that's when Mom falls in love.

When Miranda picks up her shoes and lines them up against the wall, I soften a little, too.

"What else can I make the three of you? Spritzers?" Mom gushes.

"No, Mom, we're good."

She stands at the edge of the room, beaming at us.

I'd like her to leave now. Go for a walk outside, maybe. I try to say all of this telepathically and with a pointed look toward the door. She doesn't seem to get it.

"I'll take a spritzer," Saanvi says.

So while I pluck my eyebrows out hair by hair (not really), my so-called secret society eats, drinks, and makes merry.

Eventually, I can't stand it.

"Mom, we're going out for a while," I announce, standing and pulling Saanvi up with me.

"But . . . the chocolate . . . ," Saanvi says.

"Oh, I'll get you a container," Mom says.

I force myself to smile.

"Thank you for your hospitality," Miranda says on the way out the door.

Worst. Criminals. Ever.

When we finally make it downstairs, we find Lou glowering at us.

"He made me show my student card on the way in," Miranda whispers.

"Lou! This is Miranda. She's my guest."

"Dangerous world out there. Can't be too careful. And that one looks like trouble," he says.

Which is somewhat true. Miranda obviously changed right after school. She's paired her heels with a denim skirt and a crop top. The outfit doesn't exactly say "investigative journalist."

"Don't mind him. We're leaving anyway. C'mon, Miranda."

I lead the way down the block. Then, with a quick glance

along the sidewalk (only one guy at the far end, checking his phone and paying no attention to us), we veer toward the shrubs and the "No Trespassing" sign.

I glance back to see Saanvi nibbling on a fingernail. Miranda's holding a notebook and pen as if something crucial could happen at any moment.

"Where are we heading, Dom?" Saanvi calls.

"You'll see." I lead them along the orange plastic fence that divides the empty lot from the rest of the street.

"I know I said you were the big boss, but are you completely, absolutely sure that we shouldn't head for a coffee shop? One with double-caramel macchiatos?" Saanvi asks.

I shush her.

"Ew!" Miranda squeals. "I stepped in mud. Is this going to ruin my shoes?"

I glance at her heels, purple with tiny pompoms on them.

"You don't have to come. We can fill you in later," I say.

"I'll go in front and find where it's safe to step," Saanvi says.

I roll my eyes at her, but she doesn't seem to notice.

Grabbing Saanvi's hand and leapfrogging between grass patches, Miranda manages to make it through the fence without losing what exists of her wardrobe.

And, finally, we're in. It's gratifying to hear their gasps.

"This is so super-amazing!" Saanvi squeals—quietly. There's a great blue heron poised at the edge of the pond.

"How did you find this place?" Miranda whispers.

"It's been here for years."

"The city should make it a park!" she says.

It's the perfect time of day to visit. The afternoon light is starting to fade, turning the remaining blossoms golden pink. Since I was last here, a carpet of white and purple crocuses has bloomed.

Without me directing them further, the girls meander through the Japanese maples to the group of large stones by the edge of the water. They each choose a perch.

Then they look at me.

My mouth suddenly goes dry, but Saanvi reaches to press her sneaker against mine. I decide the best way is to plunge, as if I'm diving into the overgrown pond.

I look straight at Miranda. "I've been painting some graffiti in the hallways, to draw attention to the problems caused by cameras in our classrooms, and by the school's social media policies."

"That was you?" Her eyes widen.

I nod.

"I loved the thing about the panopti . . . whatever," she says.

There's a crack from the direction of the fence and we all leap to our feet.

Someone wearing a hoodie . . .

"Holden!" My voice is embarrassingly close to a squeal, but whatever. No one notices, anyway. Saanvi and Miranda hug him. He gives me a shy wave.

"Nice entrance," I say, as he chooses the rock beside mine and we all sit down again. "You've decided to join us?"

He shrugs. "Just think how excited my mom will be when she hears I'm doing group work."

"I'm sure this is exactly what she has in mind . . ."

We're interrupted by a ding, which seems extra loud and out of place in the overgrown garden.

Miranda pulls her phone from her purse, checks it, and stands.

"I'll be right back."

"What? Where are you going?"

We watch her hop daintily toward the fence. Then, a moment later, we watch in stunned silence as she returns . . . with Max. As usual, his camera's slung around his neck.

We all leap to our feet again.

"What is *he* doing here?" Saanvi demands.

"He can help," Miranda says.

"Absolutely not," Saanvi says.

Max throws his hands in the air as if he's facing a SWAT team. "Whoa. Anyone ever told you guys you're not great at hospitality?"

Saanvi literally growls.

"Look, it's fine," Miranda says.

I frown at her. "It's not really fine, Miranda. This is a private meeting and we've already told you private things." I knew involving other people was a terrible idea. "Max, we're talking about the photos and the videos. I know you covered for me that day in the darkroom, but you're still on the wrong side of this issue."

"Massively and enormously," Saanvi spits.

"He covered for you?" Holden asks.

Max smirks. "Holden's on the wrong side, too."

"I was undercover!"

"Well, so is Max," Miranda says. "He brought me information weeks ago about Josh's game, and . . ."

187

"I'm not staying. Not with someone who helped post those videos of us," Saanvi says, grabbing her bag.

"I didn't post those," Max says.

Saanvi pauses, but she's glaring at him so hard I'm surprised he doesn't burst into flames.

"Look, Josh is a show, dude. A one-man entertainment machine. And it's not like I love being stuck in class all day, so yeah—I get sucked in, sometimes."

Even under Saanvi's death stare, he's smooth. As one part of my brain is preparing to kick him out, the other part is admiring the way he stays calm under pressure. He could be useful...

"Don't pin that forum stuff on me," he's saying. "Maybe I looked at it, like everybody else. But technology's not my thing. Plus, I live with my mom and my two sisters. They would freak if I was into that stuff. My dad still lives in Hong Kong, but he'd hop a jet right back here to murder my butt. Here, look, this is his disappointed face . . ."

Max pulls his cheeks into jowls and then grimaces out at us.

I have to fight against a smile.

Saanvi's not won over.

"So you stood around while Josh posted the videos. Does that make you innocent?" she asks.

"Well, yes. I told him that one of you and Holden was mean, but Ana had already put it together, and Josh thought it was hilarious, and—"

"Wait . . . Ana?" Saanvi interrupts.

"What does Ana have to do with this?" I say, at the same time.

"She's not exactly a fan of yours." Max raises his eyebrows

at me, as if this is obvious. "How do you think she got her own video removed?"

"SHE TRADED HER VIDEO FOR MINE?"

"And mine?" Saanvi echoes.

"Yours wasn't part of the original trade," Max tells Saanvi. "She just made it for fun."

I knew something was up with Ana. But I'm so appalled by the pure evilness of that, I have to plop back down on my rock. "What in the whole gargantuan universe did we ever do to her?"

Miranda shakes her head. "You didn't know? Max is right . . . she kind of hates you. I think she's a bit . . . competitive? And maybe jealous?"

"Of what?" Saanvi spits.

"She doesn't have a lot of friends, and you guys are always shutting her down."

"She wants my friends?" I ask.

"We're always what?" Saanvi looks just as confused as I am.

"I kinda thought she must have a crush on Holden or something," Max says. "That would explain the Saanvi and Holden video."

Holden puts his hands out, as if to say he can't help it if the world falls in love with him.

Argh. We're supposed to be focusing here. And not on Holden's many conquests.

Fortunately, Miranda's talking again. "See, Max has already brought you valuable information. Can we get on with this meeting now?"

Everyone looks at me. But I'm not the only one whose video went viral. I turn to Saanvi. "What do you think?"

She pauses for a long moment.

"I drew the beavers," Max blurts.

We simultaneously turn to stare at him.

"Beavers?" I have no idea what he's talking about.

"You know, the one by the library, and the two by the janitor's room?"

"Those were beavers?" Saanvi says.

"They're from *The Lion, the Witch, and the Wardrobe*. That's my favorite book," Max says. "Remember how the beavers help Lucy and Peter and Susan escape the secret-police wolves?"

He is full of surprises. I can't help smiling at him now. And the beavers from *The Lion, the Witch, and the Wardrobe* are a perfect response to our White Witch of a principal. I wish I'd drawn them.

"I wore a really big hoodie, and I did them as fast as I could," he says. "So they didn't turn out perfectly, but . . ."

I look to Saanvi.

"He brought us cheesecake in the caf that day. And it wasn't poisoned," she mutters.

Which is something, but not everything. "If we let you stay, will you be playing for both sides, or for our side?" I ask Max.

"Your side," Max says quickly. "Look, I started hanging out with Josh when I got to The Mitch a couple years ago. We're both on the basketball team. But you guys are my sort of people. If you'll have me, I'm totally in."

I point to his camera. "Absolutely no pictures of this meeting."

"No problem, dude."

I have to admit, he's kind of adorable, in an overgrown-puppy sort of way. Maybe he did end up in Josh's crowd because the rest of us didn't bother to welcome him.

"Fine. Let's get on with things."

I can't believe there are five of us now. At this rate, we may as well invite all the neighbors and maybe a few random strangers from the street.

"Okay, can you tell us what we're doing here?" Miranda prompts. She has her pen ready.

This time, I dive in without thinking. "We're planning more street art."

Max lifts one eyebrow. "More?"

"As in, breaking the law?" Miranda asks.

"It's not too late to leave," Holden tells them.

"Holden, don't be mean," Saanvi says. She moves to sit closer to Miranda.

"I posted the squirrel with Josh's face," Miranda blurts.

There's an audible chorus of gasps.

"That was awesome," Holden says.

Wow. This group has all sorts of secrets.

I look around the circle. "It's not too late for anyone to leave. We're going to do this the right way, and it's going to be big."

"This is great," Miranda says, already taking notes. "I'm not leaving."

I glance at Max.

"All in," he says.

A siren sounds close by, and the heron finally takes off from the pond in a frantic flapping of wings. It's possible this is a sign, and we should all go home. But then we'd be letting them all get away with it . . . the school, Josh, Ana.

"I've been reading about this British street artist named Banksy—"

"What's a street artist?" Max asks.

"Graffiti," Holden says.

"It's not graffiti! Well, it's kind of graffiti. But with a purpose. Like a mission . . ."

That sounds stupid. I mumble to a stop.

"Tell them about the stuff Banksy's done," Saanvi prompts.

Deep breath. "Well, there was this one he did in Britain, right underneath these huge security cameras on the side of a building. The cameras there are called CCTV, and he wrote *ONE NATION UNDER CCTV* in giant block letters on the wall. And even though the cameras were right there, no one could identify him."

My hands are waving around while I talk but I can't stop them and, after a few minutes, I don't want to. I tell them about Banksy's pictures of migrants in Paris. I tell them about the truck he filled with moving, squealing stuffed animals, apparently on their way to a slaughterhouse. The "Sirens of the Lambs" drove all over New York.

"If he can create all those works without getting caught, we can evade one school security system and do something huge at the open house," I finish breathlessly.

For a minute, they all stare at me. Even Holden is leaning into the group.

Saanvi looks around. "We're thinking Banksy must have assistants. Like a team of secret agents keeping a lookout, or photographing his work."

Saanvi's the only one who knows my plan so far. After Holden left us in the library yesterday afternoon, we sorted through a lot of details.

I nod. "Miranda, we're going to need press coverage, or

everyone might ignore the art, and the school will cover it up again."

"I'm on it," she says. She's wearing a Cheshire-cat grin, and I find myself grinning back at her before I can stop myself.

"If this goes big enough, I can get my mom involved," she says.

"That would be seriously amazing," Saanvi says.

"What about me? What can I do?" Max says.

It's possible we've asked a Labrador retriever to join our secret-agent team.

"You can take photos."

"You said no pictures," he says.

"No pictures *today*. Obviously we're going to need shots of the work in progress and some of the finished piece. We'll post them with Miranda's write-ups and give them to any other media people we can reach."

When he clears his throat, I brace for more excuses.

"Dude, I think we could make this even, um . . . ," he says.

We all stare at him.

"Bigger?" Miranda says finally.

He nods. Silently.

We wait.

"Alright, bud. What's your plan?" Holden prompts.

Max quickly sketches out his idea. He's only known about the project for two minutes, so of course he doesn't have the finer points worked out. But it's a good concept. It's a really good concept. I can see everyone getting excited as we all throw in our own suggestions.

"I'll have to talk to Ms. Sutton and change my project idea, but I think she'll go for it. Assuming we don't tell her all the details." He grins.

"So, we'll use the three videos," Holden says. "Dom's, Miranda's, and Marcus's."

"We should really ask Marcus," Miranda says.

"He hasn't been at school since the whole forum thing blew up. I think he might have quit The Mitch," I tell them.

"Because his fly was open? That's a bit of an overreaction," Holden says.

I remember the way my stomach felt like it had disappeared the morning he and Saanvi showed me my video. And I think of how shy Marcus always seemed.

"It might not seem like a big deal to you, but to him . . ."

"Okay, let's get back to the main plan," Saanvi urges.

Marcus is quickly forgotten as we talk details. This is going to be mind-blowing. This is way more impressive than even Saanvi thought possible.

"We need a full press strategy," Miranda says. "I'll have to bring the blog back to life, and find a way to promote this."

"Good luck with that. I think Principal Plante hates you," I say.

When Miranda smiles, it's not her regular good-girl smile. This version's kind of evil. "Yeah, but Saanvi's a computer genius, right? And we're going to need to access the foyer cameras anyway, for Max's plan. I was thinking if we had administrator access to the blog, and if Principal Plante didn't . . ."

I can see Saanvi considering. "Loop the foyer cameras, so no one sees what we're doing, and steal back your blog access."

We all wait for her verdict.

"I need to get onto Principal Plante's computer."

I need a paper bag so I can sit in a corner and breathe into it like a cartoon character.

But then Holden's asking Max something about timing for a meeting, Saanvi's talking to herself, Miranda's frantically scribbling in her notebook, and even though we're all still sitting in the abandoned lot, I can feel this thing ballooning bigger and bigger.

This is what I wanted, I remind myself. I wanted something too big to ignore.

"Can we have a super-secret-society name?" Saanvi asks.

"No," Holden says.

"The Banksy Five," she suggests, eyes sparkling.

I look at Holden, waiting for him to bail again, now that she's given him the opening. He doesn't.

"You're definitely in?"

"Someone has to keep you all from disaster," he says. "Besides, most of you are height challenged. You need me."

I smile across at him, and then we're all grinning at one another like idiots as the sun fades and the heron swoops back to the pond's edge.

For the first time, I think we might have a chance.

I wander up the stairs to my building, my head still spinning. If we're going to pull this off, there are a thousand things to plan, and—

I'm about to click my key fob and open the glass doors to the lobby when I spot George inside, standing at the concierge's desk with a fifty-dollar bill in her hand. I watch as she passes it to Lou. After he tucks it into his shirt pocket, he leans forward to say something. George pats his cheek, the same way she does to Pierre at La Patisserie.

What is going on? I can't imagine anyone wanting to pat Lou's cheek, and I can't see any reason for George to be giving him money.

I pull open the doors and catch up to my grandma at the elevator.

"Hello, darling! How was your study group?" She smiles as if I've single-handedly brightened her day.

I try to stay immune. "George, why did you give money to Lou?"

Her smile flickers. "Oh, well, a little tip. He works hard, that Lou."

Lou does not work hard. He does sudoku all day.

There are puzzle pieces in my brain again. Piece: George knew about Frank and I didn't tell her. Piece: she knows when Holden and Saanvi visit. Piece: she always seems to know when Mom's out late.

The elevator arrives and I follow my grandma inside. Though we both face forward, I can see her reflection in the mirrored wall.

"Did Lou tell you I was at a study group?"

"He mentioned you'd left with a group of kids from school, darling. I probably assumed the study group part. Why all the questions?"

I hesitate. I can tell she's lying. But am I brave enough to accuse George? Just blurt it out?

"Because I don't really believe you, I guess."

It appears I am. Maybe I'm turning into Saanvi.

"Dominica, that's—"

She stops as the elevator doors slide open. Mom's been cooking. I smell bacon as soon as we step into the hallway.

"You're just in time, Dominica!" she calls when I open the apartment door. "I'm trying a new frittata recipe."

"George is here," I call back. "And she's been spying on us."

"That's rather hasty," George says.

Mom appears, wearing oven mitts. "Did you say spying?"

"She's paying Lou to keep an eye on us."

"Really, Dominica," George sputters. "You've jumped to conclusions."

This is true. But I can tell by her face that I've jumped to the correct conclusion.

"That's how she knew about Frank, and that you met at yoga class."

"You didn't tell her?" Mom asks.

I shake my head. We both turn to stare at George.

Then the fire alarm goes off. Literally.

"Oh! My bacon!"

Mom runs to the stove. George races to open our windows, and I grab a couch cushion to flap at the smoke detector. Mom joins me with a second cushion, and—finally—the noise stops.

We have a moment of relieved silence before someone bangs on the door.

"I'll get it," Mom says.

George and I stand in the hallway as she swings open our front door and thanks Lou for checking on us.

"Just a bit of bacon," she says.

"Dangerous world. You can't be too careful."

"Oh, one more thing, Lou," Mom says, as he turns to go. "Your arrangement with George will no longer be necessary."

Lou flushes the brightest shade of magenta I've ever seen.

"I'm not sure the strata council would approve," Mom adds. "I assume you agree?"

He has to clear his throat twice before he can speak.

"No problem," he says.

"Wonderful."

He begins to turn away.

"Oh, wait one moment!"

Poor Lou. The look on his face says he's expecting some new form of torture.

"I'll send you downstairs with some scones. I'd offer you frittata, too, but it's going to be a little while . . ."

As Mom keeps Lou in agony, I follow George into the living room. She sets to work rearranging the couch cushions.

"I wanted to make sure you were safe," she says, not looking at me. "It's only the two of you, and for a long time you were so young and your mother so busy . . ."

I get it, sort of.

"I'm not that young anymore," I say.

George's eyes are wet when she turns to me. I'm so shocked, I almost forget to stay mad.

"You're all grown up these days," she sniffs.

When Mom joins us, there are apologies from George and a few more tears. Eventually there's a group hug, and everything seems as if it might be okay.

Although I don't think George will be quite so psychic in the future.

CHAPTER SIXTEEN
NORMAL PEOPLE

MY PHONE buzzes just before midnight, pulling me from sleep. It's a group text from Max.

> **MAX:** What do we do at school tomorrow? Do we pretend not to like each other? Or do we sit together at lunch so we can plan things?

> **SAANVI:** No planning while we're at school.

> **MIRANDA:** Agreed. Too dangerous.

> **HOLDEN:** It's midnight, bro.

> **SAANVI:** I think we should act normal.

> **MAX:** 😨

> **ME:** If it's a secret society, we can't sit together in the caf.

> **SAANVI:** Maybe eventually we can. Not yet.

> **MAX:** Okay, that's what I thought.

SAANVI: Goodnight.

MAX: Goodnight.

I feel terrible. Are we really going to pretend we're not friends? I don't think I can watch Max hanging with the orangutans.

ME: Wait!

ME: Max, you're going to talk to Ms. Sutton, right? About your project? Let's ask her to make it a group project.

HOLDEN: Argh! No more groups!

ME: It will give us an excuse to hang out.

MIRANDA: I'm in!

HOLDEN: Three's enough. Any more will seem weird.

MIRANDA: Can you convince Ms. Sutton to let us work together?

ME: Let's talk to her tomorrow morning. Meet at her classroom before homeroom?

MAX: kk

SAANVI: Night!

MIRANDA: Night!

HOLDEN: Shut up, all of you.

SAANVI: Goodnight, Holden.

ME: Goodnight, Holden.

HOLDEN: 💀

In the morning, Max, Miranda, and I crowd around Ms. Sutton's desk.

"Well, this is a nice surprise," she says. "What can I do for you?"

"We're wondering if we can use class time for an extra-credit assignment," I say.

"And work together," Max adds.

Ms. Sutton raises her eyebrows at him, probably wondering if he's blackmailed Miranda and me into this situation, but he's already laying out some sketches of his—our—project proposal.

I have to tamp down my excitement. Even though Max is only showing his own part of the artwork, not mine, I can see exactly how it's going to fit together.

"It's an exploration of the individual and the collective," he explains, as he points to the portraits that make up the shapes in his sketches. "All of these people are unique, yet together they form the school community."

He's a surprisingly good liar.

"And what inspired the three of you, exactly?"

I've got this one. I looked it up last night. "A Dutch photographer named Rineke Dijkstra . . . I have no idea if I'm saying that right."

Ms. Sutton smiles encouragingly.

"She frames her photos like seventeenth-century paintings, but all her subjects are modern teens. She has a whole series of them on the beach and—"

"Our subjects will be wearing their clothes," Max says.

Miranda and I both turn to him.

"I'm just clarifying," he says. "I know about that photographer. Some of her people are naked."

"Moving on," Ms. Sutton says. "If I agree to the three of you collaborating, how will you divide the work?"

"I'm the photographer's assistant, and I'll help with the written report," Miranda says.

"Dominica?"

"Um . . ." I can't exactly tell her about my part in all of this.

"Dom's also writing the report," Miranda says. "And adding her own spin to the artwork."

"Her own spin?"

"We'd prefer to keep that a surprise for now, Ms. Sutton." Miranda smiles at her the same way she smiled at my mom as she complimented her cheekbones.

Ms. Sutton nods. "I think this sounds marvelous."

Who knew she'd be convinced by the combination of Miranda's flirting, Max's puppy dog eyes, and my obvious confusion?

"So . . . we're hoping to use one wall of the foyer for the

installation, and display our work at the open house," I say. "Do you think we need Principal Plante's permission?"

I hold my breath, and I can feel Max and Miranda doing the same.

Ms. Sutton glances at the camera above the doorway. The corners of her mouth tighten, almost imperceptibly. "I'll take care of it. I think she'll like this particular idea."

And we've done it! There's nothing left except to leave the classroom and survive Max's stinging hand slaps.

"We're in business!" he shouts.

"You were amazing," I say.

He blushes ultramarine violet.

Even though three of us are now officially working on a project together, lunch is still weird.

Holden, Saanvi, and I sit at our regular table, struggling to remember what we talked about before our minds were entirely filled with protest plans. Max walks by with Josh and gang en masse, as always. Their shouting and jostling seems to fill the entire room. But then, as they pass, Max turns back and winks.

Only Miranda ignores us. She sits at her usual table full of girls, a book propped open in front of her tray. There's a dribble of ketchup on her chin.

"Stop staring." Saanvi nudges me.

"This is crazy."

"I know. But good crazy."

Good crazy.

"Is that a thing?"

"Of course!" she says.

Holden dips one of his fries into my ketchup.

"Okay, good crazy is a thing."

"Do you guys want a mint?" Saanvi offers, holding out a small tin.

"A toast!" Holden declares, once we're all holding one. "To good crazy!"

We click our tiny peppermints together.

Good crazy is a thing. That's what I'm going to tell myself for the rest of the week. Because I know things are only going to get more out of control before this project—hopefully—comes together next Wednesday afternoon.

Good crazy is a thing. Good crazy is a thing. Good crazy is definitely a thing.

We're on our way back to homeroom when Miranda appears and steers Saanvi and me into the girls' bathroom.

"I still need computer access. As soon as possible, if I'm going to get the word out," she says. "We have to get Saanvi into Ms. Plante's office."

Saanvi stops fixing her hair and she shudders. "That woman scares me. And I don't scare easily."

"We need a time when she's not there, obviously," Miranda says.

Saanvi glances my way through the mirror. "Dom, did you know Banksy might be a woman?"

"What?"

"I read a whole article about it. Pretty convincing, too. I'll send it to you."

"No surprise," Miranda says. "All the best collaborations are done by women."

Who knew I'd one day be collaborating with Saanvi and Miranda in the girls' bathroom?

"So . . . the principal's office?" Miranda prompts.

"What about Ms. Marcie?" I ask. "She's *always* there."

"Maybe we go during an evening event," Miranda says. "Ms. Marcie leaves at 3:15."

"A basketball game?" Saanvi suggests.

Miranda shakes her head. "The principal pops in and out of those. We need something that will distract her for a while. How long will it take for you to get into her computer, Saanvi?"

"We'll need her passwords."

"Old people always write them down," Miranda says.

"Then only a couple minutes, once we find them."

The bell rings. We're going to be late for homeroom.

"When?" Miranda prompts.

"We'll figure it out," I promise as we leave. "I'll figure something out."

While Mr. Nowak drones on about the Pythagorean theorem, I go over the open house plan in my mind. We have only one week to prepare, and it needs to be perfect.

We're going to paint the school motto—*Securitas Genera Victoria*—in scrolled black letters across the largest wall of the school foyer. Max, Miranda, and I will do the painting during class time, since Ms. Sutton has given approval for our project together.

Max has another job, too. This is the big addition that he suggested the first time we met as a group. He's going to take tons of portraits, and we're going to collage the images together within the painted words so the whole motto is made up of the faces of Mitchell Academy students. He's promised their faces will tell our whole story, even without the rest of the artwork.

Below the portraits, on the white expanse of the wall, we'll project three still shots taken from the forum videos.

We're going to hang black theater curtains on either side of the motto, to frame it. And hidden beneath the curtains, ready for the big reveal, will be my contribution to the evening.

I haven't even *started* the stencils for my part, so I'm not going to think about it right now.

I take a deep breath. Focus.

Miranda's busy with her press releases and media contact lists. Holden will borrow a projector from his mom. Saanvi will make sure the security's offline for the afternoon, so we don't get caught in the middle of our preparations. And she'll get Miranda access to the blog . . . but all of this depends on me getting her inside Ms. Plante's office.

That's our biggest challenge. I can't stop thinking about it, and it must show on my face. Maybe there's a special expression that says, "I'm planning criminal activities." I look up to find Mr. Nowak's eyes boring into me.

"The square of the hypotenuse is equal to . . . ," he growls.

"The sum of the squares of the other two sides."

He grunts, maybe surprised I had the answer ready. But I swear, Pythagorean theorem is a breeze compared to our plan for the open house. If we pull this off, they should study our work in all future Mitchell Academy classes.

Maybe I should thank Mr. Nowak. It's because of having my eyes lowered, trying to escape his scowl, that I notice the ripped poster on the hallway floor after math class. It's for Monday night's PAC meeting.

That's only two days before the open house. It wouldn't give us much time. If it didn't work, our whole project would be in jeopardy. But if it did work . . .

The PAC meetings involve all the bigwig parents like Saanvi's dad and Max's mom, plus Principal Plante. It's exactly what we need—an evening when the school's open, but the principal's away from her office. If we can make sure she's distracted for long enough, Saanvi can get onto her computer, adjust the security cameras, get blog access . . .

We need an excuse to be at school during that meeting.

As soon as the idea occurs, I can hear my own heartbeat in my ears. What excuse could we offer for attending? Someone would have to stand in front of Ms. Plante and all those parents and say something remotely convincing, plus warn us if anyone leaves the library and heads for the office.

"You okay?" Holden asks, when I sit down in humanities.

"You look tired," Saanvi says.

"Just thinking."

"About what?" Holden asks.

Fortunately for me, Mr. Lee chooses this moment to begin our lesson on symbolism. Not that the lecture stops Holden's guesses. The first note arrives on my desk within minutes.

YOU'RE MOVING TO MEXICO AND NEED YOUR TRANSCRIPTS.

I shake my head, smothering my smile as Mr. Lee scans the classroom.

Another note. *YOU'RE JOINING A RELIGIOUS ORDER AND TAKING A VOW OF SILENCE.*

Which is a tempting idea, except that I can't go two hours without talking and Holden knows it.

YOU'RE TURNING VEGAN AND STARTING A SAVE-THE-ANIMALS CLUB.

I roll my eyes at him, but there's actually something to that last note. Obviously, no one who's tasted my mom's pineapple meatballs could ever go vegan. But what about some sort of club? We could present to the PAC about launching a student organization. They love that sort of thing.

What was Saanvi talking about last week, when she threatened to write to the board of directors? Something about consulting the student body.

Mr. Lee interrupts my brainstorming by passing around a photocopied story and giving us ten minutes to find examples of rivers symbolizing the passage of time.

I get through a paragraph or two, and then find myself staring at the empty desk in the front row. Marcus still hasn't returned to school. No one's consulted him about technology or security issues.

"What do you think of a technology advisory group?" I whisper to Holden.

Holden looks at me as if I've suggested eating lunch from the dumpsters this week.

"We need to distract Principal Plante and the PAC on

Monday night. That way, I can get Saanvi into her office and onto her computer."

"What does that have to do with technology?"

I obviously need to slow down. "We'll do a presentation to the PAC about a technology advisory group. That'll distract Ms. Plante and keep her in the meeting. Meanwhile, Saanvi and I break into her office."

"Wow. Risky."

"I know."

"But parents will love the technology advisory thing," he says. "They'll drool over it."

"Great. Because you and Max will be presenting."

Now he looks like *he's* going to eat lunch from dumpsters. But, shockingly, he nods.

"You'll do it?" I can barely believe it.

"Do you have a problem with the assignment, Ms. Rivers?"

Mr. Lee has the most annoying ability to materialize directly above my desk. Which, in this case, is occupied by the photocopied story and my mostly blank notebook.

"Sorry," I mumble.

"Let's focus, people."

I skim the rest of the story. Rivers that symbolize the passage of time. It's not a bad concept. I'd like to find a river that could sweep us directly to next week.

I need a stack of acetate sheets for my half of the open house project. I could ask Mom or George to take me to the art supply store, but they'd get curious. And I need a *lot* of sheets. I decide Ms. Crofton is my best bet.

I find her cleaning paintbrushes after school. I can't help but notice she's still wearing pants under her smock, instead of her usual stretchy dress.

"Ms. Crofton, I need some supplies for an art project. An extracurricular one."

"Art cannot be contained to the hours between nine and three, Dominica."

For a minute, I think this will be easier than I expected.

"However, it seems even the most artistic among us must adhere to Ms. Plante's budgets. And they leave so little room for true exploration."

Ugh. Ms. Plante doesn't even know about my part of the project, and she's still managing to get in my way.

"What if it's a really important project?"

"All art is important, Dominica. All art is vital." She taps a wet hand against her heart, sending multicolored water drops rolling down her smock.

I wonder if Ms. Crofton is single. And whether she'd like to meet Andrei one day. It's possible they're soul mates.

But that's not my immediate focus. I wish I were a better liar. I wish I'd spent some time thinking of a cover story. Of course I need a cover story. Did I think Ms. Crofton was going to hand over supplies without question?

I'm obviously not designed for a life of crime.

I can only think of one option. "Ms. Crofton? You know the videos that were posted on the student forums a couple weeks ago?"

She mutters something about "abomination" and scrubs harder at the paintbrushes.

"I'm thinking of creating a reaction to that. In art.

Remember in Miranda's blog article, you said that people needed to have their values realigned? I'm trying to do that."

I say all those words in a single breath. Then I bite my lip and wait.

Ms. Crofton stops scrubbing. She narrows her eyes at me. "This reaction of yours. Is it illegal? Immoral? Dangerous?"

"Um . . . none of the above?"

She waves a hand toward the supply cupboard, sending a shower of water drops onto the floor.

"Then you take whatever you need."

I grab an entire package of acetate sheets and get out of the art room before she can change her mind.

They're a pain to get home. They're too big to carry under my arm and too big to fit in my pack. I have to hug them in front of me, and then I can barely see the sidewalk.

When I finally get to the apartment, my arms feel as if they're going to fall off. But I take the clear plastic sheets to my room, clear my desk, and pull out the first one. I place it carefully over a portion of the giant sketch I've created.

Then I start slicing.

Cutting out the whiskers is a massive pain. By the time I'm halfway through, I've learned one new thing about Banksy: he (or she!) must be very, very patient. My room is littered with bits of plastic and paper, spread across the rug like confetti. It takes forever to vacuum them all up. But eventually, I have a clear carpet.

I drag one of Mom's suitcases from under her bed and roll the stencils inside. I add masking tape and our "paint" of choice. Then I'm ready.

All we need now is Ms. Plante's computer.

CHAPTER SEVENTEEN
MCFLUFFIKINS

WE SEND so many texts on Monday, I'm surprised our phones don't explode. Every time I pass Saanvi in the hallway, she looks more anxious. And Holden looks as if he's preparing for his own execution.

Max high-fives me, but Max doesn't seem to understand the dangers of this whole situation.

We meet at the school after dinner, half an hour before the PAC meeting starts. All five of us are here. No one was willing to sit at home, waiting for news.

Holden and Max are wearing dress shirts and ties. This is a first for Holden. It would be even more impressive if there weren't circles of sweat beneath his armpits.

"This was a terrible idea," he says.

"We'll be in and out before anyone knows," I say, with more confidence than I feel.

"Not the break-in," Holden moans. "The presentation to the PAC."

"Dude, aren't you an actor?" Max asks.

"I'm out of practice. And acting's different," Holden says defensively.

Miranda seems equally nervous, and Saanvi looks petrified.

"This has to work," she says. "It's less than forty-eight hours until the open house."

As if we don't know that.

"This is cutting it close. Too close," Miranda says.

"Great. So no pressure," Holden mutters.

"We only need a few minutes in the office. Ten minutes, tops," I tell him. "You don't have to talk for long."

"As soon as we're done, I'll wave from the doorway, and you can wrap up your speech," Miranda says.

"Alright." Max claps his hands together like a gym coach. "You three better disappear while we head in."

At that moment, the front doors of the school swing open. Max's mom appears, beaming at all of us.

"So nice of you to come out and support your friends!" she gushes. "We're excited to hear this proposal."

Before any of us can escape, we're herded through the foyer, down the main hall, and around the corner to the staff room. She points us to a row of seats along the back. At the tables in front of us, a couple dozen parents are chatting. Ms. Plante and Mr. Sousa, the social media consultant, test the projector.

Josh sits in the corner of the room, fiddling with his phone. He doesn't look up.

As I'm wondering if a few of us can sneak away, Mrs. LaClaire arrives. She looks even happier than Max's mom, if that's possible, and she plants herself beside Holden at the end of our row.

She leans forward to wave at me. "This is wonderful!" she says. Then she mouths a silent "thank you," as if I've finally succeeded in convincing her son to join the outside world.

The meeting's called to order. There's a brief vote to accept last month's minutes, and a quick financial summary. (The PAC has even more money than I thought.)

Josh notices us, finally. I can tell because he whisper-yells, "Lin! Hey, Lin!" across the room until Max gives him a brief wave.

"What are you doing here, man?" Josh says.

Standing by a desk at the front of the room, Max's mom clears her throat and looks pointedly back and forth between the two of them. Then she introduces Mr. Sousa.

"He's here to tell us how his company will keep our kids safe online," she chirps.

I'm dying. How are we going to get into Ms. Plante's office if we're stuck in the PAC meeting? This is not how the evening was supposed to go. I can feel Saanvi squirming in the seat beside mine, and I know every single person in this row must be feeling the same way. Except Josh. What *is* Josh doing here? Maybe he's not allowed to stay home by himself.

Despite the situation, the idea makes me smirk.

". . . the highest priority on student safety," Mr. Sousa is saying. "In the modern world, that unfortunately means a few infringements on personal freedoms. However, only the school's administration has access to our findings, and we adhere to a strict privacy policy. Furthermore, you have good kids. If they're not doing anything wrong, they have nothing to worry about."

This prompts a few smiles among the parents, as if they're silently congratulating themselves on their offspring.

There's a brief round of applause when Mr. Sousa finishes, and then Holden and Max walk to the front of the room.

Holden's fingers grip the edge of the desk as if he might fall down at any moment.

Max, on the other hand, looks as if he does this daily. "Thank you for that presentation, Mr. Sousa," he says. "You've given us the perfect segue, as we're about to discuss . . ."

Did Max just say "segue"?

". . . a way students can participate in the school's privacy and security policies. We're suggesting a technology advisory committee."

Holden has plugged in a laptop, and he flips from the introductory slide to a bulleted list. He manages to explain plans for several guest speakers and a student outreach campaign, hopefully to be funded by the PAC.

Max's mom and Mrs. LaClaire lead an enthusiastic round of applause.

"So inspiring to see this sort of student initiative," one of the parents says.

With an official vote, the PAC agrees to fund all costs for the committee.

"You'll need a teacher-sponsor, of course," Ms. Plante says, her voice like cold water on a campfire.

Max's mom gives her a smile that seems a little forced. "Surely that won't be a problem, Kathryn."

"I suppose not," Ms. Plante says, smiling twice as tightly.

They give us a final round of applause, and even though this was a fake presentation about a fake club, I feel myself flush as pink as Holden and Max do.

Principal Plante stands. "I'll walk you out."

My stomach clenches.

"No need," Max says. "We know the way."

"Right out the front door," Holden adds.

They paste on matching semi-deranged grins.

Ms. Plante goes with them anyway, and the rest of us trail after.

"I always like to support student-led initiatives," Ms. Plante says as we leave the staff room and turn the corner. "Though I wish you'd come to me first."

"Of course." Holden slaps his forehead. "We should have done that."

Ms. Plante gives him a suspicious look.

We're walking the length of the main hallway together, which is good. We won't need to avoid the cameras on either end. But in another minute, we'll be in the foyer and out the door. It will close and lock behind us.

"Bathroom," Saanvi says suddenly.

The rest of us stop walking.

"Excuse me?" Principal Plante says, turning around.

"I'm so sorry," Saanvi simpers. "It must be the excitement. It was so inspiring watching these two speak. Do you mind if we stop at the bathroom briefly? We can walk ourselves out."

"Of course." Principal Plante shakes each of our hands in turn. Finally, she turns back toward the staff room.

"Remember," she says. "My door is always open."

When she turns the corner, my knees go wobbly.

"Nice job," Holden murmurs to Saanvi.

We're in the perfect blind spot between the far camera at the other end of the foyer and the mass surveillance of the office. Ms. Marcie's reception desk is directly across from us.

"Shall we?"

Holden ushers us forward, as if he's the host at La Patisserie.

"Wait," Saanvi says. "Too many people. Way too many. Miranda and Dom, you're with me. Holden and Max, outside."

There was comfort in having all of us together, but she's right. We watch the guys push through the double doors toward freedom, and then we turn toward Ms. Marcie's desk.

I have to fight the urge to press myself against the wall, like a spy might.

"Camera," I say as we reach the desk. Simultaneously, we pull our hoodies close around our faces.

"They'll know it's us," Saanvi says for the fourth or fifth time.

"This is only a precaution. Once you have access, you'll delete the footage." Also the same thing I've said multiple times.

We head behind the desk and toward Ms. Plante's office. I check the handle just in case, but as we expected, her door is *not* always open. While Saanvi keeps a lookout, I head for Ms. Marcie's desk and hook the key ring from underneath. My hands are so sweaty, I almost drop it. The first key I try doesn't fit, and neither does the second.

"Give them to me," Miranda says, snatching them.

She's no better. As she tries another, then another, it seems like we've been standing in the full glare of the fluorescent lights for an hour.

The lock clicks.

The three of us dive inside and push the door closed behind us. For a second, we don't speak. We're all breathing hard.

"Alright, what do we need?" I ask.

Saanvi sits gingerly in Ms. Plante's chair and wakes her monitor.

"Passwords," she says. "Check her drawers, the insides of the filing cabinet, anywhere you can think." She's already peeking at the bottoms of paperweights and staplers and the back of a family photo frame.

"Hey, check it out," she says. She points to the agenda sitting open beside Ms. Plante's keyboard. There's an appointment scribbled on Wednesday afternoon.

Hair with Salvador — 3:30 p.m.

"She's getting her hair done right before the open house! That's super-perfect! I won't even have to loop the cameras for that afternoon. I'll just delete the footage from tonight and—"

"Perfect," Miranda repeats. "But we need a password."

"Don't you have some way to figure it out, Saan?" I ask. She's supposed to be the computer-genius part of this plan.

"I'm not a professional hacker!"

"Yet," Miranda says.

"Not funny." But Saanvi starts typing. At least she's trying.

I rifle through the filing cabinet, resisting the urge to read "LaClaire, Holden," and "Lin, Max," as I flip past. Although I do go back to "Arnit, Marcus" and quickly fold his profile sheet into my pocket.

"A little help here?" Saanvi whispers.

"What about a Fibonacci sequence?" I say, remembering Ana's binder.

"A what?"

"1 . . . 1 . . . 2 . . . 3 . . . 5 . . ." I reel off numbers.

"Yes! Sort of. That gets me into the forums, but as an editor, not an administrator," Saanvi reports.

Miranda's searching the wall behind the cabinet, under the desk, behind the paintings.

"Nothing," she reports from under the plastic chairs.

My fingers stop at a file labeled *McFluffikins, Fluffy*. It's so out of place, I can't help but notice. And inside . . .

"I've got it."

A long list of passwords. If we wanted, we could probably gain access to Principal Plante's bank accounts.

I pass the paper to Saanvi.

"Pet names," she scoffs.

A minute later: "We're in!"

"Great. Can we get out of here now?" I know this was my idea, but the longer we spend in this office, the more jittery I feel. Soon they'll be able to bottle my sweat and sell it as espresso.

"Hang on. Let me delete the camera footage from tonight. I've already blocked her access to the forums and the blog."

"Won't she notice?" Miranda asks.

"Hopefully not. No one's posting anymore, so she doesn't need to monitor the site."

"As long as she doesn't suspect between now and Wednesday."

"One sec . . ."

But as it turns out, we don't have one sec. As I slip the file back into place and close the cabinet door, voices sound from the outer office.

We all freeze.

"Log out," I hiss.

"Done."

Saanvi dives beneath the desk. Miranda presses herself to the wall behind the door. But where can I hide? And what's the point? As soon as Ms. Plante comes in, she'll find all of us.

There's no time. The handle moves and the door swings open.

CHAPTER EIGHTEEN
CAUGHT

I STAND FROZEN in the center of the principal's office. Outside, Ms. Plante stands beside Ms. Marcie's desk, talking to someone. It's not actually her in the doorway. It's Josh.

He stares at me, his mouth gaping. I stare back.

"They seem pleased with the system," Ms. Plante says. "Next month we'll talk about our social media plans. How many student accounts are you now monitoring?"

From the hallway, there's a murmur of voices as parents head for the front doors.

Josh looks slowly back and forth between his mother and me. I can still see Miranda, behind the half-open door. She's peering at Josh through the gap by the hinges. Her hands are pressed against the wall as if she'd like to disappear into the paint. I can tell what she's thinking. *Why is he still here? And what's he going to do?*

"Great job tonight," Ms. Plante says, reaching across Ms. Marcie's desk. Mr. Sousa leans to shake her hand.

"Let's chat about this tomorrow, shall we?"

She's going to turn and see me. Any second now.

I've forgotten how to breathe. And it's not even about getting caught in Ms. Plante's office. Standing here, I can feel this entire project slipping away. We've ruined it.

Josh glances over his shoulder at his mom. Back at me.

There's a thoughtful look on his face, and he suddenly seems younger. It's as if his ultra-cool orangutan mask has temporarily shifted.

I plead silently with him.

Hopelessly.

Ms. Plante is turning.

Josh moves away from the office door and toward the hallway. "Mom?"

My heart clunks once, then I swear it stops.

"I think I saw another one of those squirrel things in the hall near the library."

Ms. Plante makes a growling sound in the back of her throat, and then she's gone.

I almost collapse on the carpet.

Josh helped. Why would Josh help me?

I hear Saanvi let out a long, shaky breath, but I can't see her in her hiding space under the desk.

Josh returns, smirking. "So. You've been busy."

Of course he's not really helping. He's looking for ammunition he can use. Maybe blackmail material.

Or maybe not. I saw that strange look on his face.

"You don't like the cameras either."

Josh grimaces.

"You want them gone as much as I do."

I can tell by his expression that it's true.

"You'd better get out of here. Wait for me outside," he says.

He stalks into the hallway after his mom.

"Come on," I hiss at Miranda and Saanvi.

We don't hesitate. The three of us sprint for the door.

Holden has disappeared.

"He went for a milkshake," Max says.

"Milkshake?"

It seems a little early to celebrate. Especially considering we just got caught.

"His mom was all excited," he explains. "Dragged him away."

He looks at me expectantly. Saanvi and Miranda wear the same expressions. They're all waiting for me to tell them what to do next.

What to do? I feel sick. This was my idea to start with, so I suppose it's only fair that I'm the one to get caught. That doesn't make me feel better at this exact moment.

I want to beg everyone to stay with me.

Which makes no sense.

"Alright, the three of you may as well go home. I'll wait for Josh."

"Josh?" Max says.

"Are you sure?" Saanvi asks me.

I feel a rush of gratitude. I'm not going to let her stay, but at least she offered. That's Banksy-level friendship.

"Go," I tell her.

Max is still asking about Josh. Saanvi tugs him away. "I'll explain."

"Do you think we're still on? Is it happening?" Miranda asks, as she turns to follow them.

I nod firmly. "We're still on."

But I have no idea, really. I sit on the cement steps, shivering a little in the dusk, and wait for the answer to arrive.

When he emerges alone, my chest loosens a little.

"So you've got some elaborate plan? You're going to free us from surveillance?" he asks, sitting down beside me. His questions are only semi-sarcastic. His voice doesn't have quite the usual edge.

"Why is your mom so into these cameras?"

He doesn't say anything. I've probably offended him. It's always okay to criticize your own mom. It's never okay for someone else to do it.

But eventually he sighs. "When I was six, my dad said we were going on vacation and mom would come later. He stole me, basically. Then he had some sort of breakdown and we didn't leave the hotel room for what seemed like forever."

"A custody dispute!" I blurt, remembering the posters from when I was a kid. "How did they find you?"

"The maid came in one day while Dad was in the shower. I asked her to call my mom."

I struggle to connect our stern principal to the image of a mom who lost her child.

"The police came, and then Mom flew down and got me."

"And your dad?"

"Lots of therapy. I see him sometimes, but it has to be supervised. It's a hassle, you know?"

I can barely believe it, even as I hear more of his story. It's as if the kid from those missing-child posters is sitting right here. But looking at Josh, scowling miserably beside me, I can't help but realize how ridiculous my limousine fantasy was, all those years ago. Instead of seeing the fairy tale, I think about how crushed my mom would have been. If I'd disappeared, her whole life would have crumbled.

"My mom's a little overprotective," he says. "A lot overprotective."

"I guess that helps explain the surveillance."

"It's sort of my fault," Josh says. "What kind of kid believes his dad's taking him to Disneyland and his mom's coming later? We didn't even pack."

"Say the word 'Disney' to a six-year-old and he'll believe anything."

"I've been a jerk about the cameras," Josh says. "I guess I was trying to see how far I could push my mom. Or maybe make her loosen up a bit."

"What now? Are you going to tell her about the break-in?"

He tilts his head, as if considering. "Are you going to tell me what's going on?"

His usual smirk is back, but what choice do I have?

I tell him the plan. Most of it.

I have to assume he'll keep our secrets. I have to assume we're still going ahead with the project.

As soon as I get home, I unfold the yellow school profile sheet from my pocket, find the phone number at the bottom of the page, and call Marcus Arnit.

At first, his mom doesn't want to let him talk to me. When I finally convince her, I can practically feel her presence hovering behind him.

"This is Dominica Rivers . . . from your humanities class?"

"Hey, Dom."

He sounds as if he's been flattened. He's not coming back to Mitchell Academy, he says. He's going to homeschool for the rest of the year, and maybe try somewhere new in September.

His voice gets a little more animated when I tell him my plan.

"So you want to . . ."

As he repeats the main ideas, I can tell he's picturing it.

"Absolutely not," his mom says from the background.

"What difference is it going to make now?" he asks.

"Maybe a big difference," I say.

"No, I was talking to my mom. You can use my stuff."

"I don't have to. I don't want to make things worse for you."

He laughs, in an unfunny way. "They can't do anything worse than they already have."

"Come to the open house," I suggest. "You know, seize back your power and all that."

"I don't think so."

"You're sure, though? About the picture?"

"Absolutely. I want to be part of this."

We're about to hang up when he says my name.

"What?"

"Thanks. For planning everything."

I try again to encourage him to come, but he's already hung up. At least he'll be a part of it, whether he's there in person or not.

Ms. Sutton gets Miranda, Max, and me excused from class on Wednesday afternoon. We borrow two ladders and a drop cloth from the custodian, then set up along the blank

225

wall directly across from the reception desk. Max unrolls the first stencil and he and Miranda hold it in place while I wield the masking tape. My hands are shaking. It takes me three tries to rip off the first piece. At least it's easier using acetate instead of paper stencils. I should have switched a long time ago.

"How about you stand back and tell us if they're straight?" Max says.

"We don't want them straight! They need to make an archway!" My words come out fast and shrill. I sound like a cheerleading coach on energy drinks.

"Dom, this is going to work," Max says. He's calmly securing the word *Genera* to the wall. "Tell me which way to tilt the next one."

Who would have known that Max would be capable of artistic collaboration? I always thought he had the brainpower of a golden retriever. Maybe it's Miranda's presence. Even as I stand back and motion for them to move the right side of the stencil lower, Miranda laughs at something Max says. They both turn back to smile at me. A couple weeks ago, I barely knew these two. Now, anyone walking by might mistake us for old friends.

"Good?" Max asks.

I give them a thumbs-up. I don't trust myself to talk.

Max shakes up a can of spray paint just as Mr. Lee walks by. He peers suspiciously up the ladder. "I assume you have permission for this?"

"From the boss lady herself. And this is water-soluble," Max says.

Mr. Lee grunts and walks away.

"Didn't say *which* boss lady," Max whispers, winking down at me.

We do have permission for this part of the project, thank goodness. Ms. Sutton and Ms. Plante both know that we're painting the mural onto the wall, and then arranging student portraits within the words. But they don't know everything.

The foyer is full of people. Ms. Plante has seventh-graders setting up long tables, and she's personally smoothing the wrinkles from crisp white tablecloths. An events-rental van idles outside the front doors, as staff cart in trays of wine glasses and cocktail plates.

Suddenly, Ana materializes beside me.

"Nice plant," I say.

She's wearing a headband with a tiny sprig of greenery growing from the top.

"Do you like it?" She touches the headband with fluttery fingers. "They're really popular in Asia right now, and I thought it was sort of fun. A conversation starter."

I make a noncommittal sound. She's right that it started a conversation, but I'm kind of done with it now.

"Do you want help here? I could hold one of the stencils? What are you working on?"

Suddenly, I can't take it anymore. I don't know for sure how she got the video footage of me flipping my shirt in the library, but she definitely used it. And today's the wrong day to expect diplomacy from me.

"Ana, how can you think I'd want to hang out with you, ever, when you gave that video of me to Josh?"

Her doll eyes go wider than I would have thought possible.

"You humiliated me in front of the whole school. So I don't want to join your study groups, or go to your house, or work together on an art project. Ever."

Max and Miranda have frozen on their ladders. They're probably scared to move.

"I didn't know he'd post it," Ana whispers, so quietly I can barely hear her words. "I knew he'd think it was funny. I figured out that he'd posted my video, and I wanted to make friends with him and . . ."

"You need a better way to make friends." There's nothing feisty about my words. They're pure anger.

Ana makes a stuttered attempt at answering. Then she gives up, spins, and runs from the foyer.

"Whoa," Max says.

When I turn to glare at him, he and Miranda become instantly consumed with taping their final stencils into place. Then, as Max brandishes the paint can again, Miranda hurries off to get the rest of our supplies.

I take a few deep breaths and try to calm down.

It felt good to stop pretending, to tell Ana exactly what I think of her. Although I do feel a little more forgiving, knowing she didn't intend my video to turn up on the forums. A teensy, tiny iota more forgiving.

"Hurry, people," Ms. Plante calls. "I want this all done by three."

She pauses to peer critically at our paint job as Max peels back a stencil. She can't find anything to complain about—the letters look great. *Securitas Genera Victoria,* arching above the party.

She nods briskly and moves on to the silent auction items.

As the bell rings between classes, Miranda rushes back, teetering under an armload of theater curtains. Well, she's probably teetering because she's wearing sky-high white heels, but she's also carrying theater curtains.

"Got to run!" she chirps, dropping them at my feet.

Max and I pull the ladders over and, thanks to the magic of Velcro, begin fastening a long, black curtain at each edge of the motto. The effect is quite dramatic, if I do say so myself.

"Can we place the photos?" I ask Max.

He touches the edge of one of the words. "Too wet. Should we start fastening your stencils underneath?"

Mom's suitcase sits propped against the wall of the foyer, the rest of my acetate sheets still rolled inside. Our original plan was to work under the curtains and start attaching the stencils to the wall right away, but we know that Ms. Plante's heading out soon for her hair appointment. Will we have enough time if we wait?

"Too risky to start now," I decide. "Let's do it after school."

"Okay. Then we're done."

"For now," I say.

I tuck the suitcase beneath one of the curtains. I can't have anyone looking inside.

As soon as we step away from the wall, Ms. Plante puts us to work laying out bid sheets and pencils, carrying coolers of ice, and arranging coat racks. By three o'clock, the place looks fairly fabulous. As soon as the main crush of students has left, Ms. Plante heads to her appointment.

"Almost finished?" she calls as she leaves.

"Two minutes," I promise.

And she's gone.

Miranda's timing is perfect again. She sweeps through the foyer, collects our ID tags, tucks them into her purse, and heads out the door. Before anyone can notice that we're tagless, Max and I head for the darkroom.

The place seems smaller than last time, especially when Saanvi and Holden join us in the semidarkness.

It seems even smaller once Max farts.

"Gross!"

"Shhhh . . ."

I force my fingernails to unclench from my palms. Banksy must have moments like this. Moments when his hands are so sweaty he has to wipe them on his pants, but then his elbow bashes the table and he has to bite his lip to keep from yelping because he's supposed to be hiding and the air seems thick and he's quite sure he's going to pass out if he has to stay in this spot . . .

"Breathe," Max whispers.

"I can't! You made it stink in here!" But I try. Once, Banksy painted an adorable kitten in the rubble of a bombed house in Gaza. He said that Gaza was a big open-air prison where people were trapped. He wanted to draw attention to the violence there, but people on the internet were only interested in kittens.

"This seems like a movie scene," Holden says. "Maybe they'll make this whole project into a movie one day."

"Yes, I'm sure they'll make many movies about your life."

He doesn't seem to hear my sarcasm. "I hope I get to play myself."

"Is it time yet?" I whisper hopefully.

Saanvi shows me her watch. Only three minutes have passed. It won't be long, though. Fifteen minutes, I tell myself.

Twenty, tops. Then Miranda will give us the call that Ms. Marcie's left the building.

"Holden will help me with the final stencils. Max will arrange the portraits. Saanvi, you need to find the microwave."

"Got it," Saanvi says.

"Because you've told us already. About a hundred times," Max says.

He's lucky my phone buzzes before I can answer.

MIRANDA: She's gone! Foyer is empty.

"Miranda says we're all clear!"

We tumble out of the darkroom and into the quiet of the empty, after-school hallway.

"Let's go." I don't know why I bother saying it. Everyone's already hurrying toward the foyer. Once there, I retrieve the suitcase from under the curtains. I pull out Mom's giant glass bowl, which I've borrowed for the evening, and our "paint" supplies, and pass them to Saanvi.

Holden's already unrolling a stencil.

"Back soon," Saanvi says, as she heads toward the staff room.

"Don't heat it too quickly! Low power!" I call after her.

She gives me a thumbs-up.

"This is going perfectly," Holden says, passing me the tape. "Stop worrying."

I try. But I don't think I'm really going to breathe until we're finished, one way or the other.

CHAPTER NINETEEN
SHOWTIME

BY THE TIME everything's in place, we're giddy with exhaustion and excitement.

At five, we slip out the side door of the school.

"You have chocolate on your nose," Saanvi says.

When I wipe it off, I get a gob of it on my finger, which I try to dab onto Saanvi's nose. We end up in semi-hysterical giggles. Rolling their eyes at us, Holden and Max decide a burger-and-fry run is in order. Once they're back, we stand along the wall of the school, trying to eat away our nerves.

At five thirty, a news truck pulls up to the curb.

"Wow. You really came through, Miranda," Holden says.

Saanvi scrolls through posts on her phone. "PixSnappy is going crazy. The word's seriously out there now. Everyone knows we've planned something big for the open house."

It's happening.

Miranda leaves us and walks toward the first camera crew, as if she organizes this sort of thing every day.

"Okay. This is good," I say. Good crazy. I may have to pretend I'm one of those Greenpeace activists who dangle off bridges or tie themselves into old-growth trees.

"Down!" Holden hisses, and we all press ourselves against the wall as Ms. Plante's black Audi pulls into the parking lot.

Car doors slam.

"That van is—" Her voice rings across the grounds.

Then we hear Josh.

"I had no idea you were going to have news coverage, Mom. This will be great for the school."

He's covering for us. Or maybe this is really how he talks to his mom? Both possibilities seem equally surreal.

Ms. Plante's head swivels from the school doors to the news truck and back again. Even from here, I can see her eyebrows nearly touching the edge of her newly trimmed bangs. She doesn't know what's going on.

Then Miranda strides across the lawn toward her, trailed by a slim blonde in a tight-fitting teal jacket.

"Ms. Plante!" I hear Miranda call. "Can I introduce you to Rosemarie from VTV News?"

The principal visibly straightens. She puts on her fund-raising smile. "Welcome!"

The reporter asks something I can't hear.

"... a chance for parents to get to know one another, learn more about the school, and raise money for our newest programs," the principal says.

A few cars begin to arrive, and soon there are parents in suits and cocktail dresses making their way through the double doors. Small groups of students mill on the lawn. Only students whose work is being displayed tonight are officially invited to the event. But Miranda's blog post and her PixSnappy clues must be working—more and more kids arrive.

"Shall we?" Saanvi grins.

"Do we walk in together or separately?" Max asks.

"Together, man," Holden says. "It's no use hiding now. This is your work on display."

Max actually blushes (alizarin crimson).

As soon as we push through the doors, I stop, loving the way our creation looks from this distance. Max has taken fifty or sixty black-and-white portraits. Each shows a different student staring directly into the camera lens. Ana gazes out from beneath a ribbon headband. Josh's dark eyes are framed by his long lashes. Holden, Saanvi, me . . . we're all there in black and white.

Not one of the images is perfectly rectangular. They're all cut with a curve, and Max has puzzle-pieced them together to fit perfectly within the letters of the school motto. While the black spray paint is still there behind the scrolled letters of *Securitas Genera Victoria*, it serves only as the background to the portraits.

On either side of the words hang the huge black curtains. The overall effect is starkly beautiful.

"Oh, and this is our star artist, who's done the portraiture you see tonight." Ms. Plante seizes Max by the shoulders, turning him one way and then the other to meet groups of parents. Max smiles at them blankly until Saanvi joins him and begins explaining how he cropped the images to fit the words.

Another reporter arrives with a camera operator in tow, and I see Miranda right behind them, doing a secret fist pump.

"My mom's here!" she mouths to me, pointing at a striking brunette.

My mom's here, too, as it turns out. I introduce her to Max, who's managed to escape Ms. Plante. For a few minutes, I forget that we're about to stage a mutiny.

There are more students now, and at least a hundred parents. The entire foyer is a bubbling, laughing, chattering crowd, spilling onto the lawn outside.

A reporter steps in front of me, holding her cell like a microphone. "Can you tell me about some of the work on display here tonight?"

Suddenly Principal Plante appears at my side.

"An amazing achievement, isn't it?" She smiles broadly at the reporter. "As you probably know, Mitchell Academy is a school for academically gifted students. We offer them a chance to fully explore their abilities in a safe environment. As we like to say, *securitas genera victoria.*"

The reporter stares at her blankly.

"Security breeds success." Principal Plante seems thrilled with the opportunity to explain her philosophy. "In a school with strong leadership, and students with such marvelous potential . . ."

I step away slowly, unnoticed.

Around me, a few students begin to look bored. I catch Miranda as she flits by.

"Soon?" I hiss.

Saanvi and Max appear beside us.

"Let's circulate," Miranda says. "Mention that there's something to come. Call it an unveiling. Or a reveal. Something dramatic. Build the tension!"

Then she's gone.

I'm jittery from nerves and sleep deprivation, but I paste on a fake smile and join the first cluster of people I see.

"I'm so glad you're all here for the big reveal," I tell them. It's a group of sixth-graders and their moms.

"Hey, you're in one of the pictures," a girl says, pointing.

"That's me!" I chirp brightly. Who *am* I right now? "Wait until you see what's coming."

With that and another power smile, I move on to the next group.

Nearby, I can hear Holden explaining the lighting techniques. He'll probably keep people here by boring them to death, but whatever works.

Max is close, too, forcing people's attention through the power of his puppy dog personality. "This is so cool, man. Isn't this the coolest event you've ever seen?"

He may be overdoing things.

Saanvi sounds a hundred times more professional. "It's a statement about the power of our identities," she says. "What's hidden under those expressions?"

That's getting a little too close to the truth.

I talk to another group, then another. The crowd is still growing. I spot Ms. Sutton, chatting with Ms. Crofton. The two of them have their heads bent together as if they're old friends.

There are other teachers here, too. Mr. Lee and Mr. Nowak seem to be setting up a microphone and podium, presumably so Principal Plante can highlight the silent auction and the fundraising opportunities.

Suddenly, I catch sight of George near the door. I hurry toward her.

"I didn't know you were coming!"

"I heard there was an event. Isn't everyone invited?"

"Of course."

George is going to see what I've done. The butterflies in my gut immediately grow to pterodactyl size.

Before I can say anything else, Miranda barrels toward us. "It's time."

"I have to go," I tell George. Then I plunge through the crowd after Miranda. It's enormous now, I realize. There are several more news crews, too.

Miranda heads directly for the microphone. This wasn't part of our plan. At least, it wasn't part of *my* plan. But she steps smoothly to the podium as if she's meant to be there.

"Thank you, everyone, for coming this evening. Please allow me to introduce Principal Plante, who oversees Mitchell Academy."

There's a smattering of applause as Principal Plante, with a slightly surprised but pleased expression, makes her way to the front.

"Thank you," she says. "I'm happy to see you all here. I didn't expect our little open house to reach quite this scale. But our students, as you can see, are an impressive group. We're very proud of them. The safety and security they find at Mitchell Academy fosters their scholarly achievements and their creative growth."

I throw up a little in my mouth.

Ms. Plante launches into a full fundraising spiel before she steps away. She parts the crowd, shaking hands as she goes.

Miranda manages to reclaim the microphone.

Saanvi gives me a little push from behind.

"What?"

"Go! Miranda just introduced you!"

I stumble toward the front. I can do this. I didn't expect the podium or the amplification, but I know what I have to say.

237

I manage to introduce myself. At first, I'm too close and the microphone crackles. I back up a half-step. "As Principal Plante said, Mitchell Academy is a secure place. A very secure place. In fact, there are more than thirty cameras in the hallways and classrooms, tracking student movements. We believe those cameras are interfering with open class discussions, and even affecting what our teachers choose to teach. This art installation is an expression of our concerns. Saanvi, are you ready?"

She takes a plastic vase and a white cloth off one of the cocktail tables, revealing a projector underneath.

I nod to Max and Holden.

It's time.

They each seize one of the thick ropes running alongside the theater curtains. A tug, and the Velcro releases. The curtains swoosh to the ground, revealing the rest of the artwork underneath.

There's an uncomfortable chuckle from the crowd.

Now, on either side of Max's portraits, my artwork is visible. Two massive squirrels in body armor (I couldn't resist) peer down at the school motto. Just as Max promised, the expressions in the portraits seem to change, now that the squirrels loom above them. A moment ago, the students' faces looked thoughtful, pensive. Now, they look frozen, scared, or trapped.

"How did he do that?" whispers Saanvi, who's joined me behind the podium.

I shake my head. I can practically feel Max quivering in excitement. My own stomach clenches as I wait for the final portion.

I can see Ms. Crofton and Ms. Sutton staring back and forth between the artwork and me. They seem shocked. Or maybe mad? I can't tell.

The lights go out.

Someone squeals and several people gasp in the split second before Saanvi flicks on the projector. The wall is bathed in light. Below the school motto, there are now three still shots glowing from the wall.

One shows Marcus, his fly open and his shirt flap sticking out.

One shows me, with my shirt half-off, the corner of my bra just visible.

One shows Miranda in mid-trip, her books flying.

A wave of concerned murmurs rolls through the room.

Saanvi pokes me in the back and I step to the microphone again. "These images were shared without students' permission. As you can see, there are certain downsides to security. We believe that one of the purposes of tonight's open house is to get donations for new surveillance initiatives. As students, we worry this is disrupting our education and our freedom."

"Amazing," someone says.

"Powerful."

Applause begins, first a few sporadic claps and then a swell of noise throughout the room. I'm relieved to see Ms. Crofton clapping. Ms. Sutton doesn't seem mad. When I catch her eye, she nods to me.

I don't get to say anything else at the microphone. I'm quickly surrounded by reporters, students, and parents, all shouting questions. Max flicks half the lights back on. Saanvi quickly passes around our press release, with the story of this spring's hacking incidents, as well as statistics on national school security.

I look at Holden and grin. I can't stop grinning. Who knew it was so much fun to break the rules?

"Have you, personally, been affected by security breaches?" a reporter asks.

"I've been affected by breaches, and by the security cameras themselves. That's me, flipping my sweater . . . ," I begin.

I'm distracted by Principal Plante striding toward me. The crowd parts to either side, but reporters press in to fill the gap.

"Is it true that Mitchell Academy has more security cameras than—"

"Of course not. That's ridiculous," she sputters.

"Are you concerned about the effect on student privacy?"

Principal Plante slows. She pulls herself straighter, steps past me to the microphone, and clears her throat.

"As many of you know, Mitchell Academy is a school for gifted children. However, giftedness often comes with its own social-emotional issues. Some of our students struggle with relationships. Some with authority. Recently, several of our students have seriously violated our school policies."

"By accessing security footage?"

"By accessing school grounds unsupervised, by interfering with our security cameras, and by gaining administrator control of our systems. I'm afraid this is a case of some troubled young people vying for attention."

Miranda appears beside me. "She's changing the narrative," she whispers in my ear.

"What?"

At the podium, Principal Plante shakes her head sadly. "Of course, we must treat these students with compassion. But we also have to act swiftly, especially when they're damaging public property and possibly themselves."

"She's trying to shift attention to an entirely different issue," Miranda hisses. "She wants to take control of the story."

"But we'll tell people—" Saanvi starts.

Holden puts a hand on my arm.

Mr. Nowak appears behind us. "Dominica. Holden. Saanvi. Principal's office. Immediately."

His voice sends shivers down my spine.

"Let's go," he says.

Miranda steps forward, but I shake my head. There's no sense in more of us getting expelled. As far as Ms. Plante knows, Miranda was simply acting as an MC tonight.

Mr. Nowak barrels a path through the crowd and we follow like prisoners. I feel a hundred eyes on my back as we pass below the painting and behind Ms. Plante's podium.

"Do you consider this vandalism?" a reporter calls to the principal.

"I certainly do."

I follow Mr. Nowak past Ms. Marcie's desk, through the door to the principal's office, and toward my doom.

A moment later, I hear the click-click of Principal Plante's heels.

"Really, I'm shocked at the three of you," she says, shutting the door behind her.

"You should be shocked by whoever posted those videos," Saanvi says.

"This goes far beyond the defacement of school property." Principal Plante taps a few keys and turns her computer monitor toward us.

"Mitchell Academy has a zero-tolerance policy for drugs of any kind. I've already forwarded this to your parents and the police. You may consider yourself expelled."

On screen, Holden, Saanvi, and I are toasting with tiny white mints in the cafeteria.

She reaches to click another button and the three of us appear again, this time popping tiny pink pills. We look ridiculous, eyes half-closed and mouths gaping as we toss the things at one another. One moment we're way too close to the camera; the next minute, we're barely in the frame. What are we doing? I recognize my living room couch in the background.

"Those are NOT drugs," Saanvi says.

And then I understand, finally.

"Principal Plante, how did you get that footage? That's from *inside* my apartment."

It was taken weeks ago, when Holden and Saanvi came over to sample cupcakes and we threw pink sparkle candies at each other in the midst of our sugar craze. She must have somehow accessed the webcam on my school laptop.

Ms. Plante ignores me, ignores Saanvi's protests, and launches into a lecture about respect and responsibility. Holden slides down in his chair, tilts his head against the seat back, and gazes at the ceiling. Personally, I can't stop staring at the principal. Is she serious? This whole thing is ridiculous, and yet I can still hear the word "police" echoing in my head.

I think I hear Ms. Sutton's voice outside the door. Saanvi's family is definitely out there. Her dad demands to see the principal, and I can hear her grandma talking at a million miles a minute. Someone shouts a question. We can hear Mr. Nowak struggling to maintain order.

"It sounds as if your parents are here. Shall we ask how they feel about you experimenting with drugs?" Ms. Plante asks Saanvi.

Poor Saanvi. I glance over at her, expecting to see tears. But she's gripping the arms of her chair so tightly, her knuckles are white. "You can invite them in. I look forward to explaining," she says.

I'm so impressed. If my chest were a helium balloon, it would float me up to the stratosphere right now.

"Those are not drugs." I repeat Saanvi's words, looking directly at Principal Plante. "And filming us in my house is a serious privacy violation. It's illegal."

I have no idea if it's actually illegal, but it must be, right? And as I say those words, the office door opens and Mr. Nowak steps inside, followed by a uniformed police officer. It's as if I conjured her. Or it's as if my worst nightmare has come true. I'm not exactly sure.

Holden doesn't move from his slouch.

"Holden," I hiss. He could say something in his own defense.

He shrugs. "What are they going to do?" he whispers. "Expel me? My mom's already putting me in a different school."

Still, his eyes follow the officer as she crosses the room to stand beside the principal.

"I'm Constable Marion," she says. She has strawberry-blonde hair smoothed into a low bun at the base of her neck, below her cap. Blue shirt, dark pants, a belt heavy with a baton and a gun. She shakes the principal's hand, but then she shakes ours as well. I barely manage to wipe the sweat from my palm onto my skirt.

"I understand we have a situation?" she says.

We all start talking at once.

"I'm sure you noticed the graffiti outside . . . ," Principal Plante says.

" . . . delinquents . . . ," Mr. Nowak says.

" . . . some sort of power-hungry witch hunt . . . ," Saanvi says.

"We need someone to listen," I say, but of course no one's listening. Except Holden, maybe. He winks at me, but he doesn't sit up.

Constable Marion isn't impressed. She holds up her hands and, without seeming to try, makes her voice heard above the babble. "One at a time, please. Principal Plante?"

The principal gestures toward her computer screen. "As you'll clearly see in the videos, these students have been taking drugs. Our school has a zero-tolerance policy, and there are the legal issues. And the health issues, obviously. We're highly concerned about their safety."

Saanvi snorts. "She used a school laptop to film us at home." She glares at the principal. "Do you flip between cameras, to spy on your students?"

Constable Marion holds up her hands again, because it's obvious the room is about to erupt. We wait while she watches the videos. Then Ms. Plante displays several screen grabs showing us painting the foyer and testing the projector.

"We had permission to paint the motto," I say.

"How do you explain the drugs?"

That's when my mom bursts in. She literally bursts through the door, ignoring Mr. Lee, who appears to be trying to stop her. She stands on the threshold, with Saanvi's parents peering over her shoulders. Mom's cheeks are flushed, her hair is flying around her face like a mane, and I'm sort of surprised she's not wearing a cape.

Holden regains postural control. "Your mom is awesome."

In her hands, Mom holds an industrial-sized bin of pink decorating candies, which she drops in front of Principal Plante. A few escape through a crack in the plastic and roll across the surface of the desk.

"These are from my catering company," she announces.

Constable Marion snorts. She then claps a hand over her mouth and coughs, but I'm fairly sure it's an attempt at snort cover-up.

"I received your videos. They are the most ridiculous things I've ever seen," Mom says.

"One of them was taken illegally through my laptop webcam," I add.

Saanvi grins at me.

"Taken through a child's laptop," Mom says, "without her knowledge or the consent of her parent."

"Complete violation of privacy," Saanvi adds.

But Mom's not finished. "My partner is a civil rights lawyer, and I assure you, he's more than willing to take this issue to court."

I love Frank. I'm sorry I ever doubted him. If Mom wants to marry him, or run away with him to a desert island, that's totally okay by me.

Constable Marion is peering closely at the video on Principal Plante's monitor. "May I have a copy of this?"

Principal Plante looks as if she's swallowed something rancid.

"Dominica, Saanvi, Holden," Mom says.

We pop out of our chairs like soldiers called to attention.

Mom nods to Mr. Nowak. "I'll take this matter from here," she says.

And we march out of the room.

Saanvi is immediately enveloped by her family. There are so many questions from her mom and dad, and so many tears from her grandma, I'm not sure she'll ever escape. But then her dad turns back toward Ms. Plante.

"Were you aware I'm the chair of our city council's citizen privacy committee?" he asks sternly.

I can't stay and cheer—Mom is sweeping Holden and me toward the foyer. When we pass the reception desk, we find the crowd still gathered. Everyone immediately swivels toward us.

Miranda plows forward. "I've given them the background. But they need to hear from you now."

"You're kind of . . . vibrating."

"I know," she gushes. "I've lost all journalistic objectivity!"

"Dominica, we need to go home and talk about this," Mom says.

"Can she have one minute?" Miranda's tugging me toward the podium.

Mom's stern-parent face is morphing toward glare. It's not very often she glares.

Holden steps between us. "Ms. Rivers, that was amazing," he says. "I knew you had skills, because chocolate cupcakes, but this was a whole other level."

He glances over his shoulder at me and mouths "Go."

And I do.

Miranda shoves a piece of paper into my hands. "Your speaking notes. I would have kept going, but it's so much better coming from you. Since this was your idea."

I step to the podium again, in front of the microphone, and it's as if I'm on TV. Reporters cluster around me, the crowd pressing in behind them.

"What prompted this action?" one calls.

"Could you spell your name for the record?"

"What do the giant squirrels signify to you?"

Miranda nods encouragingly. I spot George nearby, and she's beaming. Mom and Holden are watching from the steps now. Mom's lips are pressed together, but she's not glaring. Holden gives me a quick thumbs-up.

I glance down at Miranda's notes.

Explain camera issues.

And then I'm talking. I tell them about the cameras at Mitchell Academy, and the security breaches, and the way the principal controls the teachers and the class discussion.

"We believe that our ethics teacher, Ms. Sutton, was asked not to address privacy and security issues in class. As students, we've been threatened with suspension for suggesting the school address security breaches."

I don't need Miranda's notes. I have a whole list of examples.

"How many students were involved in this protest?"

"There was a group, but some might like to remain anonymous," I tell them.

Saanvi steps up behind me. I don't know how she escaped her family, but she stands at my shoulder and nods to the crowd.

I almost fall down when Holden joins her.

Miranda and Max step up beside them.

"Tell them about Banksy," Miranda says.

This is the second item on her list of speaking notes.

"When we learned about a British street artist named Banksy, and about his—"

"Or her," Saanvi says.

"Or her reactions to surveillance, my friends and I got inspired. We wanted to try our own version, to draw attention to the situation."

I have to pause for a breath. This is a lot more attention than we expected.

"Resorting to a criminal act seems extreme," one of the reporters says. He has a gray comb-over and bushy, furrowed brows.

"I wouldn't exactly call it criminal," I say.

"You wouldn't call defacing your school a criminal act?"

Before I can explain, Max steps away from the rest of us.

"Check this out!" he yells. Even without the microphone, his voice carries.

Jogging a few steps to the wall, he gives the foot of a squirrel a lick. A huge, slobbery lick, as if he's eating an ice cream cone.

There's a murmur of confusion.

Max wipes his mouth, then faces the reporters.

"Chocolate! It's delicious!" he yells.

There's a burst of laughter. People press closer to the piece for a better look. Once you know, it's obvious it's not spray paint. It's melted dark chocolate.

Saanvi leans toward the microphone. "It wasn't easy getting it perfectly smooth using only the staff-room microwave," she says.

She deserves the scattered applause that breaks out.

When I look across the crowd, I see George is laughing. So is Saanvi's mom, who's standing with her arm linked in George's.

We're triumphant. I answer a few more questions, but now that everyone understands that the "vandalism" was done with chocolate, the atmosphere is much friendlier. Once I've stepped away from the microphone, I tell one of the journalists about the school laptop, and about how Principal Plante captured video footage in my home.

"It has to be illegal," she says.

"That's what I thought."

Nearby, I can hear Saanvi telling another reporter about the video of her, and how quickly it circulated.

Max is practically buried in fans, and he's never looked happier. Holden's surrounded by girls as he explains the best ratio of dark chocolate to butter for this purpose. One of the groupies has her hand on his arm. But as I watch, he looks up and scans the room until his eyes land on me. He smiles.

My heart just about cracks open. And then it explodes when I see Ms. Sutton. There she is, holding court for three separate reporters, with a news camera zoomed in on her face, and she looks as if she was born for this moment.

"Cameras in the classrooms might seem like a good idea,

but this is an age when kids need to explore their identities. They're already hesitant to put their opinions in the world. When those opinions are being closely watched by the administration . . . well, it feels like the censorship of their ideas."

The reporters ask more questions, their voice recorders extended toward her.

I jump as someone touches my arm. It's George.

"I knew all those books would pay off one day," she says.

"You're not mad?"

But I don't even have to ask. She's wearing a gigantic smile that stretches practically from one pearl earring to the other.

"I've never been so proud."

Then Mom is there, and Frank!

"I called him. I hope you don't mind," Mom says.

They have their fingers tangled together, as if they're teenagers.

"It sounded like you needed help, but I see you have everything under control," Frank says.

"Would you have rescued me?"

"Of course he would have! Like a knight in shining armor!" Mom says.

Frank blushes, which is kind of sweet. "I'm not sure about the knight part, but I think you'd have a strong case with those laptops. In fact, you could still pursue it—"

"Not now, Frank," George says. "We can talk legal matters later. Wouldn't you say it's time for a drink? Maybe dinner?"

Mom and Frank agree immediately, but I hesitate.

"George, I feel like I should stay."

The reporters are finally heading back to their vans, but the place is still crawling with students and parents. Miranda waves at me frantically from where she's standing with Ms. Sutton and Ms. Crofton.

"Of course, darling, I understand," George says. "This is your big show."

It feels like that. I find myself smiling as I leave my family—my enlarged family—and make my way toward Miranda. Despite the lack of champagne flutes, this feels like my very own gallery opening. And I'm going to make it count.

The five of us are finally heading for the door when we run smack into Holden's mom and dad, who've obviously driven here without looking in the mirror. His mom's lipstick is outside the lines and his dad's normally coiffed hair is squished on one side, like he just woke up from a nap. They're both breathless and wide-eyed.

"The school emailed," his dad says.

"We're supposed to speak with the principal, immediately," his mom says.

"I thought you were on a work trip," Holden says. "Shouldn't you still be on the plane?"

"We finished sooner than we thought," his dad says. "Took an earlier flight. What *is* all this?"

Their eyes flit back and forth between the giant motto and Holden, then to Saanvi and me, then back to Holden. The last news crew is still packing up. A few students are taking photos.

"Did you have something to do with this?"

"I guess." Holden shrugs. "It was a group project. The one I mentioned, with the art?"

His mom throws herself at him and wraps her arms around his neck. "I'm so proud of you!"

"Now, I don't know if that's necessarily appropriate." His dad does a much better job of normal parent reaction, but I barely hear him. Because the look on Holden's face . . . it's as if he's in one of those horrible movies when an alien has taken over someone's body and, on screen, the face flits back and forth between alien and human. Holden's face is flickering between happiness and horror.

"Honey, we should still probably speak to the principal." His dad tries to gently pry his wife's arms from his son.

"Oh, I wouldn't bother. She's with the police," Saanvi says.

"The police!" Holden's mom gasps. "Maybe the three of you went overboard, but surely this is a school matter . . ."

"It's not about us," I assure her. "At least, not like that."

When I glance toward Ms. Plante's office, I see Josh leaning against the reception desk. I guess he's waiting for the police to finish interviewing his mom. He doesn't look happy, but he nods to me. We're good.

Then Max bounds up. "Are these your folks? Do you guys want to see the art close up? Ms. Sutton has cordoned it off so no one damages it, but she let me show my parents, because I was one of the creators."

Saanvi rolls her eyes, but it's hard not to smile as Max leads the way.

Holden's mom hurries forward.

"You're a friend of Holden's, right?" she asks Max.

"Yeah. I'm going to get him on the basketball team next year. We'll have a blast."

When Holden's mom looks back at us, she's positively glowing.

I catch sight of Ana, then, and it seems as if things aren't going quite as well with her parents.

"This is exactly the sort of thing we've been talking about," her mom says. She has arched, plucked brows and high cheekbones. Any sense of humor has probably been liposuctioned out of her. "Why weren't you involved in this?"

Ana flaps her hands and manages a few vague words.

"If you want the university of your choice, this is exactly the sort of thing in which you need to participate," her dad says.

I stop to smile at her. "Oh, she did participate. Didn't you, Ana?"

I feel a tiny bit bad when she bursts into tears and runs off toward the bathroom. I feel a little worse when her mother strides after her, still lecturing.

"Her mother seems horrible," Saanvi whispers as we walk away. "We may have to be nicer to Ana."

I consider. "Maybe. We can try."

Shockingly, I am feeling sympathetic. "Do you think she'd have posted that video if I'd been nicer to her in the first place?"

"Nothing gave her the right to post that."

Which is completely true. And I can't promise to join any science study groups. But I resolve to be at least a little more patient with her in the future.

Saanvi and I find ourselves alone in front of the entrance and I plop onto the top stair, my legs suddenly shaky.

"We did it."

"We killed it." She grins.

For a minute, we sit quietly, listening to the murmur of voices from inside.

Then she turns to me. "I never had a crush on Holden," she blurts.

"Okay . . ."

"In that video? I wasn't staring at him."

"Well, maybe they edited—"

"I was staring at you."

I am officially shocked into silence.

"But I don't feel that way anymore," she says quickly. "I mean, I still love you to bits. Bits and pieces. But Miranda and I are kind of—"

Miranda emerges at that moment, shaking hands with the last of the reporters, as if she does this sort of thing on a daily basis. She gives us a cheerful wave and disappears back inside.

"That's amazing," I manage. "Miranda's great."

"I know. And now you and Holden can—"

"Wait. I thought Miranda liked Holden."

Saanvi rolls her eyes. "Why?"

I try to remember. The head massage in ethics class? But I guess a head massage doesn't necessarily equal love.

I shake my head. "I have no idea."

Saanvi starts rhyming about me and Holden sitting in a tree, as if she's six years old.

I laugh. "Maybe. He has a few issues to work out."

She grins back at me. "No kidding."

I don't want to think about all of that just now. I stand and pull Saanvi to her feet. "Let's have one last look at our work."

It's pretty incredible. Max is still snapping photos. I'd like to send some to Banksy. Maybe we can post them somewhere. And I want print copies, too, to remember all this.

There's one other small moment I'll remember.

While Saanvi's talking to Max, Holden steps up beside me and links his pinkie in mine. His fans seem to have headed home, finally.

"Can we get out of here for a minute?" he asks.

We push through the double doors and wander down the stairs, toward the corner of the building. Automatically, I check the map of cameras in my mind. I tug Holden a bit farther from the entrance.

He scuffs a toe in the grass, like a little kid. "Did Saanvi tell you about her video? I mean . . . about Miranda?"

I nod.

"My mom says I can stay at The Mitch."

"That's amazing!"

When he looks up at me, he seems almost as nervous as he did before his speech to the PAC.

"Everything's okay then, right?" I say.

I think everything's more than okay, but it's possible I'm misinterpreting this situation.

Or maybe not.

Holden steps closer to me. He hooks a piece of my hair and tucks it behind my ear.

"Can I . . ."

He leans in at the same moment I nod, and he ends up kissing the end of my nose.

I'm not sure which one of us readjusts, but the second kiss lands where it's supposed to. My stomach does a full Fibonacci spiral.

There aren't any cameras where we're standing along the side of the school. There aren't any news crews. Max and his telephoto are safely inside. There's no one here at all, except for us. This moment won't be appearing on the forums, or on anyone's social media feed. Because this moment is private. Perfectly, better-than-I-could-have-imagined private.

CHAPTER TWENTY
BRAVE NEW WORLD

THE REST of the week is a blur. It's as if we've lit a rebellious spark in the school. The teachers barely manage to keep control of their classes. In art, Ms. Crofton launches a unit on murals. I notice she's wearing one of her clingy bamboo dresses again.

In ethics, Ms. Sutton gives up on what she had originally planned. She starts a class debate on privacy and security instead.

I don't see her glance even once at the camera in the corner.

The voices in favor of classroom privacy far outweigh those in favor of security. It would be interesting to hear what side Josh would support . . . except he's not at school. No one's seen Ms. Plante, either.

"Can you text Josh and ask where he is?" I whisper across the aisle to Holden.

"You hate Josh, remember?"

"Hate's a strong word. And I'm curious."

"All I can think about is cupcakes," Holden says.

Miranda is twirling a strand of Holden's hair around her finger, and I don't even care. "Mmmm . . . cupcakes," she says.

Normally Ms. Sutton would have shushed us by now, but she's lost control again. Everyone's talking.

Holden's obsessed with my mother's baking plans. "How many flavors is your mom making?"

"Six."

"And two of them are different varieties of chocolate," he sighs happily.

We all head directly to Holden's house after school. Our parents are going to join us at dinnertime.

It seems our parents have done a lot of talking. Max's and Holden's moms were especially horrified by the shots stolen from the school security cameras, since the PAC had helped fund them. As the news spread about Ms. Plante spying through our laptop cameras, there was a flurry of parent texting and phoning.

Holden's mom finally invited everyone—Saanvi's family, Max's parents, Miranda's parents, Mom, and even George—to her house to "discuss the situation." Then mom offered to bring cupcakes, and ever since . . .

"After-dinner dessert extravaganza."

Holden can only think about cupcakes.

I roll my eyes, but it's kind of nice sitting here on the couch with him, our hands linked. Max and Miranda have commandeered the video game controllers and they're in the midst of an intense racing game. Saanvi's tucked in a corner chair with a book, but she's reading with a smile on her face. Every so often, she glances over at Miranda.

After a while, I hear parents start to arrive. We go upstairs, say hello, and dish ourselves pizza. I notice that Holden manages to get a caramel cupcake onto his plate, even though they haven't been served yet.

"Do you want to go in?" Holden asks, pointing toward the living room. It's a babble of adult voices.

I consider for a moment, then I shake my head.

"I feel like we've done our part. They can take it from here."

"Think they can handle it?"

"We should at least let them try." I grin. "How else are they going to learn?"

We stay downstairs until the cupcakes are officially served. Then Holden has three more.

On the Monday morning after the open house, people are still talking about it. We're like heroes in the school hallway. Even Josh's posse gives us fake bows as we pass, though Josh is still nowhere in sight.

Saanvi and I roll our eyes at them.

"Where's your fearless leader?"

"Moving," one of the orangutans says.

"Moving?"

"Yeah, they move a lot, man," another says. "This is like Josh's third middle school or something."

"Sucks, dude," the first one says.

I don't feel at all sorry for him when I think of him as Josh. But when I think of the kidnapped kid caught up in a custody dispute, there's a twinge. I guess everyone has issues.

"I think Ms. Plante got fired," Saanvi whispers as we walk away.

When Holden and I go to ethics after homeroom, there's an unfamiliar teacher standing at the front of the class with Ms. Sutton.

"This is Ms. Tran. She'll be taking over the class for the remainder of this semester."

"Where are you going?" Ana, of course, has her arm raised toward the ceiling.

"I'll be taking over as interim principal while the board decides on a new direction for Mitchell Academy. Ms. Plante has decided to seek another position."

The class erupts in cheers and high-fives, and Ms. Sutton doesn't bother reprimanding us.

"Are the cameras coming down, Ms. Sutton?" Miranda calls.

"I think that's likely," she says.

This time, I even high-five the posse.

After class, we sit at our regular cafeteria table. But it's not just the three of us anymore. Miranda and Max seem to have permanently joined the group. And today, when Ana walks by, I make myself call her over.

"Do you want to sit with us?"

Her eyes widen, and she immediately plunks down her tray.

"Do you want to talk about the humanities assignment? Get a head start on it?" she asks.

"No, Ana. Let's just have lunch."

"And cupcakes!" Holden says. With a flourish, he pulls a plastic container from his pack and sets it in the center of the table.

"What's this?"

He pulls off the lid to reveal a dozen slightly lopsided efforts, decorated with a wide variety of sprinkles.

"Dude, you made these?" Max has already grabbed one.

"I have found my calling, thanks to Dom's mom," Holden says.

"Your calling is cupcakes?" Miranda laughs.

"My parents have already signed me up for a baking class. At my request."

I can only imagine how happy Holden's mom must be.

I take my time choosing. Eventually, I pick the one in the center, with the red and white heart sprinkles. Holden touches the edge of his to the edge of mine, as if we're clinking champagne glasses.

Miranda sighs happily. "The future's looking bright," she says.

"And free of surveillance," Saanvi says.

"Full of art," I add.

And also full of cupcakes.

A NOTE ABOUT CYBER BULLYING

Dom and her friends decide to tackle their cyber-bullying issues themselves, which is a great strategy for adding action to a novel, but not the best strategy in real life. Dom's first step should have been to talk to a trusted adult: a parent or teacher, for example. Schools take incidents of cyber bullying very seriously, as do internet providers and police forces. To learn about steps students can take to prevent or combat cyber bullying, visit:

http://www.rcmp-grc.gc.ca/cycp-cpcj/bull-inti/index-eng.htm

http://cyberbullyhelp.com

AUTHOR'S NOTE

Banksy, the street artist who inspires Dominica, is a real person. As Dominica writes in her project proposal, he began painting graffiti in Bristol, England, and has since created art all over the world. The works referenced in this book are also real, as is his film, *Exit Through the Gift Shop*. Banksy remains anonymous. However, there are places to see his (or her) work. The best source is Banksy's own website: www.banksy.co.uk.

Kriston Capps wrote about the theories that Banksy is a woman, or a team of artists led by a woman, here: www.citylab .com/design/2014/11/why-banksy-is-probably-a-woman /382202/.

ACKNOWLEDGMENTS

Banksy, whoever you are, thank you for highlighting social justice issues, for pointing out the absurdities in our world, and for inspiring this book.

A big thanks to all the people who helped this novel come to life, including my agent, Amy Tompkins. None of my books would ever be finished without my fabulous writing group, the Inkslingers: Rachelle Delaney, Kallie George, Sara Gillingham, Stacey Matson, Lori Sherritt-Fleming, and Kay Weisman. I'm completely in love with Lynne Missen and Peter Phillips at Penguin Random House Canada, who seem to get even my lamest jokes. Thank you also to copyeditor Linda Pruessen, who worked with me on both this book and *Eyes and Spies*— we are now experts in all things surveillance-related!

Thanks to my beta readers, Shae, Adelaide, and Julia. (Adelaide and Julia are also the creators of the two-legged giraffe texts which I blatantly stole.) And most of all, thanks to my cheerleading squad: Min, Julia, Matthew, Shirley, Gordon, Sandy, Jason, and Moe.